MRS. MAY IS WELL AND TRULY DEAD

A WELL AND TRULY MURDER MYSTERY

SANDY C. MCKEE

TRU
STYLUS

Published by: Tru Stylus, LLC

ISBN 978-1-957067-01-8

CONTENTS

1

CHIEF ARLEN WELL SPOTTED TWO MEN STOMPING TOWARDS THE Hutton Village police station. He pivoted into the village store and watched through the window as they jockeyed for position to enter the front door.

"Avoiding the mayor and councilman, huh?"

Arlen smiled a greeting at Joe Solina, the store owner. "Your future son-in-law can handle them. Good training for when I retire."

Joe snorted, "You're a long way from retiring, Arlen. And Sergeant Cashel Truly, blast him, is a long way from proposing marriage to my Ana Sofia."

"They're young. I'm sure he'll get to it."

"Ha! Three years of Sunday dinners and what do we have to show for it? Nothing! Maria, God rest her soul, would have had them married with our first grandchild on the way by now."

Arlen glanced at the framed photograph of Joe's late wife that hung on the wall behind the counter. "Maria was the best of us."

Joe nodded, "Yes, as was your own dear wife. They are sorely missed."

The two widowers observed a companionable moment of silence. Joe cleared his throat and gestured to the counter.

"Got a new hair dye in stock. Plant-based, no chemicals. Think I'll try it myself. What about you? Cover that little bit of silver on that thick head of yours. The village ladies would love to see you with darker hair."

Arlen scoffed. "My hair is thick, but my head is not. The ladies of the village, with all due respect, can mind their own beeswax. Besides, I think a bit of gray makes me distinguished."

"That's about right, I reckon."

A timer dinged from the back room. "Sausage and cheese muffins are done. Mind the store and I'll fetch you one."

Joe disappeared into the back and Arlen took a seat in the little circle of chairs in the middle of the store that Joe kept for his customers and neighbors to visit. The combination market and dry goods was the only place to shop in Hutton Village. There were no restaurants, so Joe's was the place to grab a quick snack. The other option was candy from the vending machine at Nate's Garage on the other side of the village square.

On the rare occasion when an outside traveler took a wrong turn and found themselves stranded, they would be fed and housed by one of the villagers. The adventurous visitors found this charming; the less intrepid were shocked and sometimes horrified. Regardless of the reaction, village hospitality never waned.

"You want some coffee to wash it down?"

"Let's see how bad it is first." Arlen bit into the warm, savory muffin and sighed. "As close to perfect as it gets."

Arlen polished off the muffin, then put some money on the counter. "If it's more than that, put it on my tab."

"We don't charge city prices here. Besides, that was a gift. Take back your money."

"Can't do it. Might cause a scandal, you trying to bribe a peace officer."

Joe laughed and rang up the sale.

Arlen glanced at his watch and sighed. "I'd better get to the station. Truly will be in over his head by now."

"Nothing new!"

Arlen pulled his jacket tight and stepped into the crisp, chilly courtyard of the village square. The business district, such as it was, consisted of several free-standing buildings facing each other across an expansive lawn. It was open to pedestrian traffic only and served as the venue for the popular seasonal village festivals.

Mercifully, the morning rain stopped, however, the ground was covered with frost. The withered frozen grass crunched under Arlen's boots as he made his way across the lawn. Even with his sturdy winter wear, the cold pierced through him. He consoled himself with the thought that the mayor and councilman would no doubt create a lot of heat in the station.

He entered through a side door and tiptoed to his desk on the right side of the one-room police station. Ava Corbridge, his dispatcher and office manager, smirked and wagged her finger at him. He winked, hung up his jacket, then sat down and pretended to read reports.

On the opposite side of the room, a vigorous discussion ensued with Sergeant Truly faced off against Mayor Riggs Hutton and Councilman Chesley Direberry who had their backs to Arlen. He caught a hint of acknowledgement in Truly's eyes, but the young sergeant kept a passive face.

"You haven't answered my question, Sergeant," huffed Councilman Direberry. "The Winter Festival is in two weeks! What are you doing about this crime spree?"

"I wouldn't call it a crime spree, Chesley," protested Mayor Hutton. "But it is concerning, yes, very concerning."

"Concerning?" mocked Direberry. "Don't dither, Riggs. It's a blot on our village. People are coming here from the city---heck, from all over---pouring hard-earned money into our economy. We can't have this. It's illegal and must stop! Why have laws if the police won't enforce them?"

"I'm sure they're doing their best. Right, Sergeant Truly?"

"This is the first we're hearing about this particular, um, crime spree," said Truly. "However, now that we know, going forward we will give it the attention it deserves."

He said that with a straight face. Good man.

Direberry scoffed, "I don't see how when your Chief can't be bothered to come to work! Shirking his duty and getting paid? That's theft of wages! Mark my words, at the next council meeting we will demand an explanation for why we came here--- during business hours, mind you---and found an empty--"

Direberry spun around with a flourish to point at Chief Well's desk but stopped short when he saw Arlen sitting there. Arlen smiled and waved.

"Chesley. Riggs."

"Arlen!" exclaimed Mayor Hutton. "We didn't hear you come in. Mrs. Corbridge, why didn't you announce the Chief?"

Ava turned a steely gaze on him. "I'm not a butler, Young Riggs."

Arlen noted the blush on the mayor's face at Ava's use of his childhood nickname. The mayor was the namesake of his father, Old Riggs, who in turn was the namesake of his father, Elder Riggs. Each man had been the mayor of the village in their own time, such that it seemed to be more of a hereditary title than an elected office. The villagers didn't mind. The Huttons were benevolent, albeit condescending, rulers and no one else wanted the job.

"Yes, well…" the mayor stammered, then turned his gaze on Arlen. "You could have said something!"

"It's not polite to interrupt. Carry on telling the sergeant about your crime spree. I need to concentrate on earning my wages."

Arlen turned his attention to the papers in his hand, but out of the corner of his eye he saw Mayor Hutton kick Direberry, which was a liberty that was only allowed because the mayor was married to the councilman's sister. Direberry glared at his brother-in-law but had the good graces to look embarrassed.

"See here, Arlen," said Direberry. "I didn't mean anything by that. I'm just upset---"

"As usual." Arlen didn't look up from his papers.

"Rightly so! This is a serious matter."

Arlen set the papers down and considered the councilman. "Like the last time? Theft of your prize roses? Who did we arrest, Sergeant?"

"The councilman's goat. Insufficient evidence to prosecute, so Gruffy was released into the councilman's custody."

"I trust you mended the fence around his pen, Chesley. Against village ordinances to let livestock wander at will. Sergeant Truly, add checking the councilman's livestock to your list of duties."

Truly picked up a notepad. "Goat surveillance. Right, Chief."

"Have your laugh, Arlen. This time it's serious."

"I agree with Chesley," said the mayor.

Both men turned earnest faces to Arlen. Behind them, Truly shook his head slightly.

"Fine, gentlemen. Tell me why you think peaceful little Hutton Village has turned into a hotbed of crime. You have my full attention."

"We need you to put a stop to---"

"Chief," interrupted Ava. "Urgent matter."

"Mrs. Corbridge, really! Can't it wait?" Direberry huffed.

Arlen saw her ashen face and jumped to his feet. "What is it, Ava?"

Ava glanced at their visitors. "Rose called. I've texted both of you the details."

Truly grabbed his phone first and read the message. His eyes grew big. Without a word, he pulled on his jacket and bolted for the door.

Arlen took out his phone. *Dead body. Shot. Road west of the lake.*

"Ava, you know who to contact."

"Already done. I also texted Olivia to come in."

"Good job."

He was out the door within seconds. The mayor and councilman sat in stunned silence. Arlen trusted Ava not to reveal any details to them or the villagers until they got a handle on the case. *Dead body. Shot.* He felt a knot forming in his stomach and he sprinted the rest of the way to his car.

On an ordinary day, Arlen enjoyed driving the country roads outside the village. The foothills to the east of Appalachia were, in Arlen's opinion, as close to paradise as one could get. He still lived in the small lakeside cabin where he was born and raised. He couldn't imagine living anywhere else. As a boy, he freely roamed the forests, hills, and meadows that the village claimed within their borders. There were no major highways or freeways nearby and it was a several hours drive to the nearest city or town, which was exactly how he liked it.

"It's peaceful here," he once told his father as they sat on the front porch of the cabin watching the stars.

His father chuckled and ruffled his hair. "That it is, son. That it surely is."

Arlen gripped the steering wheel and focused on the road ahead. Today that peace was broken---with a gun. Who? Why? His chest tightened, and once he reached an open stretch of road, he floored it. As he approached the scene, he pulled in and parked behind Truly's car.

Fifty yards ahead he saw reserve officer Gavyn Pepper cordoning off a wide area by the side of the road. The young carpenter and part-time peace officer worked carefully and methodically, scanning the ground as he walked.

An obviously rattled teenage boy sat in the back of Gavyn's pickup truck with a blanket wrapped around him. A fishing pole lay abandoned beside him. Rose Tern, a landscaper by trade, and the only other part-time reserve officer for the village, scribbled in a notebook as the young man talked excitedly.

Across the road, Truly jotted notes of his own as he spoke with Dr. Jackleen Concord, the village's only practicing doctor. She treated both the villagers and their pets.

"I draw the line at livestock," she once told Arlen. "But dogs and cats…sure. They're family. Bring 'em on in."

Arlen decided to speak first to who he presumed was their witness. As he approached the pickup truck, Rose acknowledged him with a nod, then pointed at the boy.

"Timothy here was on his way to the lake for a day of fishing when he noticed something laying in the ditch by the road. Turned out to be our victim. Didn't have his phone with him, so he ran all the way to the Hutton estate and found me working in the hothouse. I called Gavyn and Ava, then had Tim show me the way."

"Well done." Arlen turned to the boy. "That must have been very upsetting, Timothy."

The boy nodded his head so hard that Arlen was afraid his brains would scramble. "It was, Chief Well! I ain't never seen nothing like it before and I don't never want to see it again! There was blood and, and---"

Arlen held up his hand. "That's fine, Tim. Let's start from the beginning."

The boy sat upright, and Arlen continued. "You planned a day of fishing, right?"

"Yes, sir."

"What're you using for bait? I don't see a tackle box."

Timothy reached in his pocket and pulled out a plastic bag. "Marshmallows. My mama taught me that."

Arlen nodded in appreciation. "Smart. What are you fishing for?"

"Heard tell of a giant trout spotted in the lake and told the fellers I'd be the one to get it and we'd have us a fish fry. They be like 'bet you only catch bluegill' and I said 'well, bluegill's good eatin', ain't it?' and they said---"

Arlen held up his hand again and Tim stopped. "Where exactly was this giant trout spotted?"

"Chief," warned Rose.

"We'll save that detail for later. For now, young Timothy Springer, answer me this. Today is Tuesday. Is there a school holiday I don't know about?"

Timothy looked at his hands. "I, um…see, um…"

"The *lure* of fishing was stronger than school. Am I right?"

Timothy cracked up. "You're funny, Chief Well. I gotta tell the fellers that one."

Rose shook her head but continued writing in her notebook.

Arlen smiled. "My fisherman's heart is with you, Tim, but there's no way I can keep this from your parents. When Officer Tern takes you home, she'll tell them that you did the right thing by getting help as fast as you could after you found the victim. That's the best we can do."

"Thanks, Chief Well."

Arlen patted the boy on the shoulder. "One more thing. Next time you feel lured by the lake, stop in the station and ask Mrs. Corbridge to show you the almanac. It would have told you today's not a good day for fishing."

"Wow, how do you know that?" The boy's eyes were big.

Arlen whispered, "I check it every day."

Rose snorted and Timothy giggled.

"Please take the rest of Tim's statement, Officer Tern, then meet me back here after you've driven him home."

"Yes, Chief."

Arlen walked to the edge of the cordoned crime scene and was soon joined by Truly who was carrying a large, sealed evidence bag. Dr. Concord paced down the road, issuing orders into her phone.

"What do we have?" Arlen pointed to the bag.

"Handbag. Victim is a white female, middle-aged. Lying face down in the ditch. Gunshot wound to the back of the head. We didn't turn her over yet. Waiting on Gavyn to take photographs after he secures the scene."

"Very good. What else?"

Truly hesitated. "I know the training you sent us to said not to jump to early conclusions, but I think I know who the victim is."

Arlen raised his eyebrows. "Who?"

"Niralya May."

"Mrs. May? What makes you say that?"

Truly pointed to a small grove of trees. "Her car is parked over there. We'll need to process that area after we finish here."

Arlen nodded. "Well spotted. Work the original scene first, as quickly as you can, so Dr. Concord can examine the body."

"Don't rush on my account," said Dr. Concord as she snapped her phone shut. "The van from the city morgue will take three hours to get here, then another three to get back. I'll gather what evidence there is, but this morning's rain and the cold snap will affect my findings."

"Do what you can, Kathleen. That's all we ask."

"Are you going to call in the state police?"

"My team can handle it. Their training is current, including homicide investigation. We send them to the city every year."

"Yes, I heard Direberry complaining about the cost at the last village meeting."

"We're doing our best to enlighten the councilman on the value of investing in training."

"Good luck with that. He's as rich as Ava's fruitcake yet will squeeze a penny 'til it howls."

"We'll solve this case quickly, Chief," said Truly. "Show the councilman. He won't fight us on accreditation after that."

Dr. Concord whistled, "You're going for accreditation? That's ambitious."

"Hutton Village is small and sleepy now," said Arlen. "But we don't know what may happen in the future. Development could come in and blow up the population overnight. Seen it in other towns. Don't want that to happen, but if it does, the team will be well equipped to handle the needs of the people."

Dr. Concord pointed to the evidence bag. "I agree with Cashel that Niralya May is likely our victim. Every Sunday when collection is taken, she makes a grand production of opening that designer purse and pulling out a thick lavender envelope. She glares at her husband, then plops it in the plate. Daxton sits there red in the face. She has all the money, you see."

"What does Mr. May have, I wonder?"

"The looks. More than one woman in the village would love to catch his eye---married or not. I blush at the excuses they come up with to talk to Niralya just so they can catch a glimpse of his chiseled jaw. I don't know if I attend services for the spiritual enlightenment or the drama! Better think on that."

"I had no idea the front of the church was so interesting. We'll have to start sitting up there, Truly."

"I like it in the back. Fewer people see me arrive late."

Dr. Concord leaned in and whispered, "The Lord sees you, son."

Truly paled and Dr. Concord laughed as she walked away to take another phone call.

"Other observations?"

Truly hesitated. "To be honest, I was hoping it was an accident or maybe a suicide. Both bad options."

"Agreed."

"But the entry wound in the back of the head and no weapon found nearby pretty much rules either of those out."

"Yep."

"Which means unless they hightailed it out of the county…"

He paused and stared at Arlen who finished the thought.

"…there's a killer in Hutton Village."

2

_____

SEVERAL HOURS LATER, ARLEN'S TEAM HAD PROCESSED ENOUGH of the crime scene to enable them to turn the victim on her back. As they suspected, it was Niralya May.

Arlen stared at the lifeless form and felt a twinge of guilt that over the years he hadn't made a better effort to get to know the Mays. Decades ago, he and Niralya had taken lessons together in the one-room village schoolhouse. She began kindergarten when he was in high school. He remembered he once pulled a box of crayons off a high shelf for her. She grabbed the box and ran away without thanking him. Later, her wealthy family sent her to private boarding schools up north. After she finished college, Arlen heard that she traveled from city to city doing whatever it was that rich socialites did.

When her parents died five years ago, Niralya returned to the village, new husband in tow, to manage her family's extensive property holdings. To Arlen, she appeared to be a reserved, yet formidable, woman. She participated in the village festivals, but never put herself forward or made demands. Neither did she allow others to make demands of her. Juniper Hutton, the mayor's wife, and queen bee of the village, tried in vain to cajole her into various subservient festival roles. Niralya stood firm and did her part on her own terms.

Arlen's thoughts were interrupted by the arrival of the city morgue van. Under the watchful eye of Dr. Concord, the attendants transferred Mrs. May quickly and efficiently from the ditch to the back of the van.

"I'll follow the van," said Dr. Concord. "If the villagers need medical attention, tell them to call Dr. Min---if he can pull himself away from his online followers. He's still a doctor even if he is averse to handling sick people. Better yet, call his wife, Jennifer. She has more sense."

"I will. Let us know your findings as soon as possible."

"Of course. I can tell you this much. One shot to the back of the head, close range, no exit wound. My guess is a .22 caliber pistol."

"Time of death?"

"This morning between seven and eleven a.m. I'll know more after the autopsy."

"Thanks, Kathleen."

Arlen and his team lined up on the shoulder of the road, hats in hand out of respect for Mrs. May, as the coroner's van drove off. After it passed, they huddled together to confer.

"A .22," said Gavyn. "Common as dirt in these parts."

"We found one shell casing by the road," said Truly. "Unless it was moved, we can pinpoint where the shot was fired. It doesn't match how we found Mrs. May---lying face down---so we're thinking the killer moved the body off the road. Perhaps to conceal it for as long as possible."

"This road is not often used," said Rose. "The killer may have thought the body would be out here for days or would attract scavengers, making it harder to find evidence."

Arlen nodded. "Didn't count on an avid fisherman skipping school today, did they? So, if they moved the body, they must be strong."

"Not necessarily," said Rose. "The ditch has enough of an incline to roll a body off the road."

Gavyn nodded. "The blood pattern on the ground backs that up, Chief."

"Let's keep that detail, and the shell casing, to ourselves for now."

"That's probably all we can keep quiet. Timothy and his family have likely called the entire village and county by now," said Rose.

Gavyn blushed. "Yeah, my phone is blowing up. I turned it off."

"Good man. Truly, call Ava to set up a whiteboard in the storeroom. Move some boxes out. It'll be tight, but that's the best we can do for an incident room. We need to keep our investigation away from prying eyes. Have Nate tow Mrs. May's car to his garage. Lock it up tight. No one is to touch it."

"I'm on it," said Truly as he walked away to make the call.

"Rose will accompany me to notify Daxton May of his wife's death. Gavyn, when you and Truly finish here, meet us back at the station."

"Yes, sir."

On the drive to the May residence, Arlen mentally rehearsed what he was going to say to Daxton May. It had been years since his last death notification visit. He glanced at Rose and saw the frown on her face as she stared straight ahead.

"Spit it out, Rose. What's on your mind?"

She hesitated. "Chances are, he did it."

"Who?"

"The husband."

"Did we find evidence of that?"

"No, but statistically speaking, it's usually the spouse."

"Let's find actual proof before we slap the cuffs on him."

"I'm just saying we should watch him carefully. Domestic spat turned deadly. Happens more than you think."

Arlen paused. "I know you had a bad experience in the past."

"I don't want to talk about that."

"No. I'm just saying that while it would be naïve of us not to keep your suspicions in mind, we need to go where the evidence leads us."

"Don't jump to conclusions, in other words."

"Exactly. Set our biases aside. Follow procedure."

Rose crossed her arms. "Agreed. Follow procedure...then arrest him."

Arlen pulled into the sweeping circular driveway of the expansive May estate and parked under a large oak tree. The majestic mansion, haughty and proud, demanded their full attention.

"Wow," said Rose. "How many columns does one house need? What's this style? Greek?"

"Beaux-Arts neoclassicism. My father did some carpentry work on it over the years, and he taught me a little about the architecture. Mrs. May's family, the Browns, moved here and had the house built in the 1930s."

"They had money during the Depression? Where were they from originally?"

Arlen stopped. "You know, I'm not sure. Near the coast, I think. They didn't mix much with the village. Brought their own household staff and shopped in the city."

"They had servants?"

"Still do as far as I know."

"Must be nice."

"Given today's events, the Mays obviously have their problems like anyone else."

"Too true."

As they mounted the stairs leading to the portico, Rose hung back. "I feel underdressed."

"What?"

"I'm wearing jeans and work boots. To enter a house like this,

I should be wearing a taffeta gown and satin slippers. Maybe a tiara."

Arlen stared. "Want to go home to change?"

Rose snorted. "As if I had anything grand enough. It's just I feel like the house is judging me."

Arlen let out a long sigh. "Rose, you're a good officer, but right now you're talking nonsense. Can we please focus on the task at hand?"

"I'm sorry, Chief. My mind races to crazy places when I'm nervous. I don't like confronting killers."

Arlen held up his hand. "We don't know he's the killer. For now, he's a soon-to-be grieving widower. The situation is quite serious, Rose. There's no room for ridiculousness."

As Arlen approached the front door, it suddenly burst open. Daxton May took one step out but stopped short when he saw Arlen and Rose. His hand flew to his mouth, he giggled shrilly, then darted back into the house and slammed the door.

Arlen raised his eyebrows at Rose who shrugged. Arlen rapped three times with the ornate iron door knocker. A few seconds later, the door opened a crack and Mr. May's right eye stared wildly at them.

"Mr. May? I'm Chief Well and this is Officer Tern. May we speak with you? It's important."

Mr. May opened the crack a few inches. "I'm not at home."

"You obviously are. May we speak with you, please?"

"I mean, I'm not at home to visitors. I'm on my way out, so if you could come back later, that'd be great."

"Mr. May, this is official business. I really must insist that we speak with you now. It's about your wife."

"Oh? In that case, yes, do come in for a minute. Let's sit in the morning room."

Arlen and Rose followed him into a bright, tastefully furnished sitting room.

"Can't offer you tea, I'm afraid. Servants' day off. Unless you'd like to find the kitchen and brew a pot for us."

He turned a magnetic smile on Rose who responded with a stone face and narrowed eyes. Mr. May's smile faltered.

"Yes, well…sorry."

"We're not here for tea, Mr. May," said Arlen.

"Please sit and tell me how I can help you." He looked at his watch, then gestured to two high-backed overstuffed chairs opposite the floral sofa where he plopped down. Rose took out her phone and placed it on the coffee table. Mr. May looked at her quizzically.

"We're recording this meeting," she stated flatly.

"With your permission," Arlen interjected.

Mr. May shrugged. "Sure, whatever."

He settled back into the sofa and looked expectantly at Arlen.

Arlen cleared his throat. "Mr. May, sadly we're here to inform you that your wife is dead. We're very sorry for your loss."

Mr. May blinked at him. "That's not possible. Niralya is in perfect health."

"She was shot, Mr. May."

Arlen heard the sharp intake of breath. "Shot? Who would---oh, my God! This can't be true."

"It is, I'm afraid."

Mr. May put his head in his hands.

"She was found late this morning on the isolated road on the west side of the lake."

Mr. May's head shot up. "Then, it's not my Niralya after all. Whew, you gave me a fright."

"We're not mistaken, Mr. May. The victim is your wife, Niralya May."

"Impossible. Today is Tuesday."

"And?"

"Don't you see? Tuesday is the day Niralya goes to inspect the east cottages and collect the rent. East, not west."

"Weekly?"

Mr. May nodded. "That's one of her little ways. Insists on collecting the rent weekly and in person. Every Tuesday---even on holidays. Afterwards, she has lunch with her friend Wandalene. Doesn't get home until late afternoon. Every Tuesday, without fail. So, you see, it couldn't be Niralya. She wouldn't be caught dead---"

Arlen raised his eyebrows.

"Sorry, I mean she would not break her routine for anyone or anything. Even me. She simply would not be on the west side of the lake on a Tuesday. Not Niralya. It's inconceivable."

"And yet, I'm sorry to inform you, she did, and she was. There's no doubt it's Mrs. May, though we will need you to make a formal identification."

Mr. May stared at Arlen as if he'd grown another head. During his stunned silence, they heard the front door slam and the clack of heels on the polished floor.

"Where's Niralya? She didn't show for luncheon. She can't still be mad."

Arlen and Rose stood as a scowling Wandalene Brackett marched into the room. She planted herself in front of Mr. May, who had remained sitting, and put both hands on her hips.

"They'll tell you." Mr. May waved towards Arlen and Rose. "I'm---I'm distraught."

He sat back and put his arm over his face.

Wandalene glanced at Rose, bowed her head curtly, then turned to Arlen. "Explain!"

"Ms. Brackett, we've just informed Mr. May of the unfortunate death of his wife."

Wandalene's face drained of all color, and it seemed to Arlen that she deflated right before his eyes. She swayed on her feet and Rose sprang up to guide her to a chair.

"Thank you, child," she said. "Dead? How? She was fine on Sunday. Was it a car accident?"

Wandalene looked from Mr. May to Rose to Arlen.

"The village will be informed shortly so I trust you will keep this to yourself until then."

She nodded as the tears pooled in her eyes.

"She was found on the road west of the lake---"

"West? You mean east?"

"I tried to tell them." Mr. May's words were muffled as he spoke through his arms.

"Regardless of Mrs. May's ordinary routine, today she was on the road to the west of the lake. She was shot---"

"Shot!"

"Yes, I'm sorry for the loss of your friend."

"Best friend," said Ms. Brackett thickly. "Best friend in the world."

"Do you know anyone who had a reason to do such a thing?"

Ms. Brackett narrowed her eyes at Mr. May but turned a passive face to Arlen. "There's really nothing I can tell you, Chief. I---I am unwell. This is too much. I'm going home."

She stood abruptly and barreled towards the door. Arlen nodded to Rose who sprinted to catch up to the older woman. Ms. Brackett allowed Rose to take her arm and guide her out of the house. Arlen turned his attention back to Mr. May.

"Mr. May, I'm sorry to intrude on your grief, but time is of the essence if we are to apprehend the shooter. Do you feel up to answering some preliminary questions?"

Mr. May nodded and sat upright. Arlen noted that his eyes were dry.

"Yes, if it doesn't take long. I was on my way out, and obviously I now have more things to do what with arranging services and the will---."

"Thank you, Mr. May. I appreciate you taking time out of your busy schedule to help us find your wife's killer."

Mr. May flushed. "Of course, I didn't mean---um, obviously, that's the most important thing."

"Exactly. Now, when did you last see your wife?"

"She left the house right after breakfast. Must have been around seven."

"Did she say anything to you before she left?"

"Nothing stands out. It was a typical Tuesday. Servants' day off, her day to collect rent, and so forth. She called out when she was leaving---I was on the phone with my friend."

"Did she say anything to you about her plans for the day? Anything outside of her normal routine?"

"No, just goodbye." Mr. May paused and cocked his head. "It wasn't really a proper goodbye, was it? Calling out as you leave the house. We take people for granted, don't we?"

"We often do. What did you do after she left?"

Mr. May bounced his right knee as he cleared his throat. "Me? I don't remember very clearly."

He stood up and walked around the sofa and began pacing back and forth, rubbing the back of his neck. "Let me think."

"It was only this morning, Mr. May. Can you not recall what you did?"

Mr. May stopped abruptly and blinked rapidly at Arlen. "I think the shock is---is blocking my thoughts. Do you mind? I'm quite parched." He pointed to a well-stocked drinks cart in the corner.

"Water or soft drinks only, please, Mr. May. Until we conclude our interview."

"If you insist." Mr. May shook his head. "Even after five years, I can't get used to this dry village. Would you believe no one serves cocktails or wine? Not even for dinner!"

He poured himself a large tumbler of water and downed it all at once. He poured a second one and sat on the couch. "Of course, when we host, we do things properly. At least on that point Niralya and I agreed. You'd better believe the paragons of this village lap it up, too!"

Rose burst in the room carrying a covered casserole dish that she plunked on the coffee table. Mr. May jumped and spilled a little water on his slacks. He frowned at Rose, but she smirked in return.

Arlen sighed. "Officer Tern, what is that?"

"A carload of women insisted they had to drop this food off to Mr. May. I told them it wasn't a good time, but they weren't having it."

"How did they know the situation?"

"Oh, they do that every Tuesday," said Mr. May. "Nova and the girls know our staff have the day off. They like being neighborly."

"I'll bet they do," said Rose. "Very neighborly to keep you company while your wife is out for the afternoon."

"What's that supposed to mean?" Mr. May frowned at Rose.

"Officer Tern let's get back to the interview, please. Mr. May is about to tell us what he did this morning after his wife left the house. He's gathering his thoughts."

Rose nodded. "Sometimes older people have trouble remembering things."

"Older!" sputtered Mr. May. "I'm barely forty-five and still in my prime, let me tell you!"

"Forty-five?" asked Arlen. "Mrs. May was fifty-three, wasn't she?"

Mr. May shot Rose another glare, then turned to Arlen. "Yes, she was a few years older, but that was of no consequence to us."

"I see. Let's get back to my question. What did you do this morning?"

Mr. May looked up at the ceiling. "I tidied the breakfast things. Niralya likes things neat and clean, and it was really no bother, so I did it. Then, I puttered around the house, went out for a bit, came back, had a late lunch, puttered some more and then....and then you folks arrived and turned my world upside down."

He struck a stoic pose and shot another glance at Rose. Her face was stone, so he turned to Arlen.

"Where did you go when you went out?"

"I had errands to do in the city---or what passes for a city around here."

"You drove all the way to the city and back before lunch?"

"It was a late lunch. Around three o'clock."

"Can you tell us exactly where in the city you went and who you saw there?"

"No place special. Just here and there. Can we do this some other time? I really do think the shock is setting in. I need to be alone."

"I understand, Mr. May. Last question for now. Do you know anyone who would wish your wife harm? Had she argued with anyone?"

Mr. May looked blankly at Arlen, then answered.

"Yes, well, maybe. She and Wandalene had a fierce argument after Sunday's dinner. I don't know the details. As usual, I went to my room after dessert and left the two of them to talk the night away. I heard raised voices but couldn't make out the words."

"I'm sure you tried your best," said Rose.

"I did. I mean, I couldn't help hearing with all the shouting. I was shocked, let me tell you. They've been pals for ages. At school together. When we moved back to the village, Wandalene followed."

"I remember that. They were obviously very good friends."

"Rather like family, I should say. Anyway, the only other disagreement was with that tenant she was evicting. What's he called? Named for a president. Washington? No, the other one."

"Lincoln? Lincoln Zader?"

"That's the one. They had a bit of a clash when she gave him the eviction notice last week. Threatened her, she said."

"She didn't report this to us."

"No, she said she would handle it herself. She and her lawyer." Mr. May shuddered.

"Mr. Zader must be nearly eighty years old. As I recall, he's lived there forty years or more. If he was behind in his rent, the village would have helped. She didn't need to evict him."

"It's not that. He always paid promptly and in full. No, Niralya got it into her head one day that she wanted the property back. I don't know why. Worthless, as far as I could see. But she always gets what she wants, doesn't she? You don't challenge Niralya without suffering the consequences, let me tell you!"

He nodded pointedly at Rose who said, "May she rest in peace."

Mr. May paled. "She's really gone, then?"

"Yes, Mr. May. I'm sorry. Is there someone we can call for you? Pastor Deighton perhaps?"

"No, no. I'll do it. When---"

He looked at his watch and jumped up.

"I'm late! See yourselves out, will you?"

With that, he ran out of the house. A minute later an engine roared. Arlen and Rose went to the window and saw Mr. May talking on his cell phone as his red sports car spun out of the driveway and onto the main road.

3

ARLEN WAS IMPRESSED WITH HOW QUICKLY AVA TURNED THEIR dusty storeroom into a functioning incident room. Decades of files and boxes of whatnots were removed, and the space was scrubbed within an inch of its life. Laptops, writing pads, and markers were neatly lined up on a narrow oak conference table. A printer and other supplies were set up on a small table in the back corner. The walls were covered with large sheets of stick-on whiteboard paper.

Arlen smiled as Ava bustled in and placed a small bouquet of flowers in the middle of the table. Trust Ava to add the personal touch.

"Ava, this is fantastic. Let's keep it like this. Might impress the accreditation team when the time comes. How did you manage?"

"Lots of help. Gavyn donated the table. He made it for some outsider a few years back, and they stiffed him on the bill. He's happy it's getting some use. The school donated the paper and markers. Joe gave us supplies from his store at no charge. My husband and Olivia did most of the work, but a few other villagers stopped by to lend a hand. Including your sweetie, Burklie. She did all the heavy cleaning. Don't worry, I didn't tell anyone a thing."

Arlen ignored her remark about his so-called sweetie and nodded. "Thank Nate for me. He's towing Mrs. May's car to his garage. Remind him to lock it up tight until we get our search warrant."

"He knows. I've trained him well. Anything else before the team gets here?"

"No. Looks like you thought of everything."

"Unlike you. Did you eat?"

Arlen's stomach growled and he blushed.

Ava put her hands on her hips. "Didn't think so. Platters of sandwiches and veggies are in the break room. Fresh coffee is brewing."

"You're a marvel."

"Known that for years," Ava said over her shoulder as she walked back to her desk.

Arlen wolfed his meal, then organized his notes while waiting for his team. Olivia Pepper, Gavyn's younger sister and the village's sole technology whiz, was the first to arrive. She nodded at Arlen, then immediately checked all the laptops.

Truly, Rose, and Gavyn followed closely behind and took their places. Ava stood at the door and scanned the room.

"Ava, lock the front door, then join us."

"Already done."

"Good. We have a long night ahead, so let's get started. Truly, report."

"Victim is Niralya May. White female. Fifty-three years old. Married."

Rose snorted.

Truly continued. "Dr. Concord gave us preliminary findings at the scene. One shot to the back of the head, close range. No exit wound, so likely a .22 caliber handgun. Time of death, this morning between seven and eleven o'clock."

Truly waved to Gavyn who jumped in. "We secured the scene. No tire tracks or footprints nearby except those matching Mrs. May's car and shoes. The location of the shell casing and the blood on the ground indicate she was shot on the edge of the road, then her body was rolled into the ditch. It's a steep incline so it wouldn't have taken much effort. My guess is the shooter parked on the road and was careful to walk only on the asphalt. May have used a long-handled tool or some type of lever to push the body."

"That's a good observation, Gavyn," said Arlen.

Gavyn blushed and looked down at the table. He took out his handkerchief and rubbed a spot.

"We recovered her purse and impounded her car," said Truly. "We'll need search warrants."

"I contacted Judge Tanner," said Olivia. "She's driving in from the city tomorrow and will stay in the village for at least a week. She also mentioned that she has plenty of time to officiate weddings while she's here."

She looked pointedly at Truly who scowled at her. Ava chuckled softly.

Rose looked horrified. "Heaven forbid. Marriage is the leading cause of divorce. Fact!"

"Let's focus on the case, if you please," said Arlen. He stood and wrote on the wall's impromptu whiteboard. "Means, motive, opportunity. Thoughts?"

Rose spoke up. "Means is likely a .22 handgun which nearly everyone in the village owns or has access to. The shell casing won't give us much. There were no prints on it."

"Good. Motive? Mr. May alluded to a couple of recent disagreements. One was an argument with her long-time friend Wandalene Brackett. We don't know what that was about. Rose, did she say anything to you when you helped her to her car?"

"No, she clammed up. Barely nodded a thank you to me."

Truly stood up. "Here, Chief, let me write while you brainstorm."

Arlen handed him the marker and returned to his notes. "The other disagreement was with her tenant, Lincoln Zader. She was evicting him."

Gavyn gasped. "Old Lincoln? That's terrible. Where's he supposed to go at his age?"

"There's a caretaker's cottage in our south field," said Olivia. "Dad will let him stay there."

"Don't worry," said Arlen. "I suspect Mrs. May's death puts a hold on the eviction. Unfortunately, that gives Mr. Zader motive. We'll have to include him in our list of suspects, regardless of our personal feelings."

Truly wrote both names on the board. "Which brings us to Rose's prime suspect, the husband."

Arlen nodded. "Yes, we have to consider him. He hasn't accounted to us for his whereabouts this morning and, shock and grief aside, his behavior was off."

"Squirrely," agreed Rose. "Lots of nuts stored in that noggin of his."

"Rose," warned Arlen. "Stick to the facts."

"Fine, but I stand by squirrely. The way he thundered out of his driveway, yakking on his cell phone. I wish I had my tag book. I counted at least four traffic violations."

Truly wrote Daxton May's name on the board. "He had opportunity unless he can give us an alibi. No doubt he has access to a .22 pistol. Mrs. May's father was a gun collector. There's probably an arsenal stored in that big house. What's his motive? Any problems between the two of them?"

The team looked at each other and shrugged. Arlen noticed Ava glancing away.

"Ava, you know something. What can you add regarding the May's marriage?"

Ava pursed her lips. "I don't like to gossip, but I suppose since it's a murder investigation…"

"Go on."

"Word is the Mays recently argued viciously over money."

Rose looked incredulous. "They have pots of money!"

"*She* has pots of money. He brought nothing into the marriage other than his pretty face and expensive tastes. She had him on a tight allowance, but he was always after her for more. They had a dust up last week in the city. Quite public, which is not like Niralya."

"How do you know this?"

"Giddy Hutton's housekeeper's niece works at that fancy tea shop in the city. She saw them going at it hammer and tongs over scones and a pot of Darjeeling. They kept their voices down, but she heard Mrs. May say 'Not another penny!' before she stormed out of the shop."

Gavyn raised his hand and Arlen nodded at him.

"Will he inherit now that she's dead?"

Rose spoke up. "Not if he killed her."

"We don't know that he did," said Arlen. "At this point, he's high on our suspect list. We need proof. Next steps are to check alibis and get a search warrant for the house and her financials. We'll see if Judge Tanner thinks our observations of his behavior and the testimony of the niece in the tea shop amounts to probable cause. Let's divide---"

Arlen was interrupted by a loud banging on the front door of the station. Ava started to rise, but Arlen stopped her.

"Truly and I will go first. Remember, there's a killer on the loose. Exercise extreme caution. That goes for all of you. Keep the door to this room locked at all times. No one from the outside is to come in here. Sorry, Ava, but that includes Nate."

"He won't mind."

The pounding on the door became more insistent. Arlen advanced and saw a heavily made-up face pressed against the glass. It was the mayor's wife, Juniper "Giddy" Hutton.

"Lovely. Just what we need," Truly whispered behind him.

Arlen unlocked the door and the queen bee of the village burst in without invitation.

"What took so long? I nearly broke a nail pounding on that door!"

"Miss Giddy, we're in the middle of an investigation. Unless you have information pertinent to the case, I'd be obliged if you would leave us. Please."

Miss Giddy's face paled. "Information? What would I know about it?"

"Then why are you here?"

"Wh-why?"

"Yes. I don't mean to be rude, but we're very busy."

Miss Giddy cleared her throat and stood up straight. "I-I thought you might be hungry. I brought some of Cook's barbeque chicken and cheese biscuits. And I wanted to remind you about the Winter Festival village-wide meeting tomorrow night. Mandatory attendance. That includes all of you."

She glanced around the station as she handed a large canvas tote bag to Truly. He breathed deeply. "Smells wonderful, Miss Giddy. Sure appreciate it."

"That's what neighbors are for," she said absently as she turned around, looking into every corner of the room.

Arlen followed her gaze. "Did you lose something, Miss Giddy?"

"No, no. Not a thing. Did you start work on the case yet? I don't see anything."

"We're working in the old storeroom, now incident room. The station is a bit...public. I'm sure you understand."

She tugged at her collar, then pinned her arms against her stomach. "Of course, of course. Well, I'll go say hey to Ava, then be on my way."

She started for the back but was blocked by Ava advancing into the station.

"Giddy! Is that Cook's prize-winning barbeque that I smell? Aren't you sweet as pie?"

"Pie!" exclaimed Miss Giddy. "I have buttermilk pie in the car. I'll bring it in a flash."

"I'll go with you, Hon," said Ava. "Save you the trip back. I swanny, sure was thoughtful of you…"

Her voice trailed as she steered Miss Giddy out the door.

Arlen looked at Truly who was rummaging in the tote bag. "That's the first of what will be many invasions."

"You can't blame folks. Everybody's rattled."

"I don't blame them, but I won't allow interference with our investigation. Well-meaning or otherwise. No one else comes through that---"

The door opened and Ava ushered in Truly's girlfriend, Ana Sofia Molina. "Look who I found."

"Hello, Chief. Hi, Cashel." Ana Sofia handed Arlen a plastic container. "Dad made pawpaw muffins."

"That's very kind, Ana Sofia. Be sure to thank him from us." He handed the container to Truly who juggled it with the tote bag.

Ava tutted, grabbed all the food, balanced the pie plate on top, and headed for the break room. "I swanny, it's not that hard," she muttered as she walked away.

"We'll certainly be well fed during this case," said Arlen. "Assuming we'll be allowed to get on with it."

He looked pointedly at the door. Ana Sofia laughed. The soft, tinkling sound reminded Arlen of the stained-glass hummingbird windchime his late wife bought on their honeymoon trip to the mountains.

"Sorry, Chief. The village isn't used to murder. We don't know what the etiquette is. When in doubt, bring food."

She gave Truly a peck on the cheek and twirled out the door. Truly blushed.

"She's a keeper, you know, Truly. Smart, too. We may need to bring her in as a consultant on the Mays' financials. None of us have an MBA, that's for sure."

"Don't I know it," said Truly. Arlen noticed a brief cloud pass over Truly's face. They didn't speak on the way back to the incident room.

At the door, Arlen stopped short. In their absence, Ava had placed linen napkins and lace doilies by each person's laptop. The doilies were topped with dainty porcelain plates decorated with a motif of coral peonies and gold rosettes. She walked around the table placing cheese biscuits and pawpaw muffins on each plate.

"Brought out the good china, huh, Ava?"

"Mrs. May would appreciate it," she shrugged. "Now mind your crumbs. Snacks only in here. If you want a full meal, use the break room. By all accounts, the village will keep it stocked."

A chorus of "yes, ma'ams" replied.

Arlen took a second to appreciate the warm, sweet muffin before resuming the briefing. "Right. We know of three possible motives, so far. Next steps, search warrants."

Olivia looked up. "Judge Tanner signed off electronically on warrants for the house, car, purse, plus financial and phone records. We did a videoconference while you and Cashel were defending the front door."

"Good initiative. Let's divide and conquer. Gavyn and Rose, do a quick search of the car tonight, then a more thorough one in the daylight tomorrow. Truly, process the purse---Ava, help him, please. Olivia, work your magic on the financials and phone. Rose, did you say the shell casing had no fingerprints?"

"It was clean. No prints at all."

"I didn't expect any, to tell the truth. This killer seems careful not to leave traces behind. At the risk of jumping to an early conclusion, I'd say the murder was premeditated."

Ava raised her hand. "When should I send the village text?"

The village group text was the method of communicating important events, festival updates, and other news. It was sent to the heads of households who would in turn inform their families. Years ago, Olivia proposed that the village get an online messaging system, however the elders of the village baulked at what they termed her newfangled ideas. They were comfortable with their phones, so they compromised by tolerating a group text.

"Miss Giddy mentioned tomorrow's festival meeting," said Arlen. "Mandatory attendance, as if we weren't in the middle of a murder investigation. Still, we can use it to our advantage. Ava, schedule an information session for an hour prior to that. Save folks an extra trip into the village."

"Makes sense. I'll send the message."

"Alright, you have your assignments. Meet here in an hour. Meanwhile, I'm going to…think."

Arlen grabbed a cheese biscuit and focused on his notes. The hour flew by. Arlen stretched his legs and stared at his empty plate as if to conjure another biscuit.

Ava bustled in and swept up the dishes. "You want vinegar pie or honey cake? We're switching to decaf coffee, but I can make regular if you like."

"It's not your job to wait on me, Ava. I can fetch my own coffee."

"Your job is to catch a killer. My job is whatever I say it is. At the moment, it's part assistant, part station chef. Don't worry. I'm keeping track. When this is over, I'll expect y'all to wait on me hand and foot."

"Gladly. What were the choices again?"

"Vinegar pie or honey cake. Decaf or regular."

"Did you make the pie or the cake?"

"Both."

"Then I'll have both. And decaf is fine."

As the team straggled in, Arlen noticed how tired they looked. The village kept early hours, even the young people. He hated to press them, but finding the killer took priority over comfort.

"Let's make this quick. What did you find in the car?"

"Cleanest automobile I've ever seen," said Gavyn. "Not a thing inside it except registration and insurance cards. No prints other than Mrs. May's. We'll search again tomorrow, but I doubt we find even a speck of dust."

"Puts me to shame," said Rose. "When this is over, I'm taking a personal day to detail my truck."

"Mr. May said his wife liked things tidy." Arlen pointed to Truly. "What did you find?"

"The purse is the definition of tidy. Contains only three items: a wallet, a journal with an attached pen, and a smart phone. The wallet matches her designer purse---both are worth more than I'm paid in a month. She had a drivers' license, one credit card, and a few dollars in cash. That's it. The small leather journal is also high quality and has a record of her rent receipts. It's new. Dates begin January first of this year. No entries for today, since she didn't make it to the east side as planned. I turned the phone over to Olivia."

Ava looked pensive. "It was odd. She didn't have any of the things normally carried in a purse. No comb, lipstick, tissue. It was all rather...businesslike."

"She was on business, collecting rent. Not a social call," said Arlen. "I expect that's normal."

"But she always had lunch with Ms. Brackett on Tuesdays," said Rose. "Wouldn't she have wanted to freshen up?"

Arlen considered. "I wonder if she planned to see Ms. Brackett today. They had an argument on Sunday. Maybe she was going to collect the rent, then return straight home. Something to think about."

Truly jumped up and wrote it on the whiteboard. He turned and pointed at Olivia. "What did you find on the phone?"

"Equally tidy and equally bizarre. Had a few apps that the phone came with, but she didn't use them. Didn't access the internet. The only contact was for the village group chat. No text or call history saved, so we'll need to wait for the report from her carrier to learn that information. My guess is that she used her home landline for calls. Maybe kept this expensive smart phone for emergency use only."

"It didn't help her today, did it?" Arlen sighed. He rubbed his temples. Two desserts had been a mistake, though they were delicious. He needed to walk off the sugar.

"It's late. Go rest up. Back here at seven a.m. Truly, swing by and pick up Mr. May and bring him in for further questioning."

"What if he won't come?"

"His options are to accompany you to the station like the concerned, grieving husband we know him to be---or be arrested for that display of reckless driving that two sworn peace officers witnessed."

"I really hope he picks option two," said Rose. "That would make my day."

4

DESPITE THE RICH FOOD, ARLEN SLEPT WELL AND AWOKE refreshed. He arrived at the station at five a.m. to find Ava and Olivia rearranging the break room.

"What are you early birds doing?"

"You need a proper interview room," said Ava. "We don't have one, so this will have to do. The break room is now in the upstairs loft. Y'all have to climb a tad, but some of us need exercise, don't we?"

"That we do," said Arlen as he watched her cordon off the sink area with a bamboo screen. The kitchen table was transformed by a dark gray fitted tablecloth. A single silk gladiolus stem in a bud vase was the only decoration.

Olivia buzzed around plugging in and testing their equipment. "We're all set with video and audio recording, Chief. I'll control it from the incident room so you can focus on your witness---or suspect."

"Thanks, both of you. This is a temporary inconvenience. Once we arrest the killer, we'll go back to our quiet, sleepy routine."

"That we will," said Ava firmly. "Despite what Councilman Direberry thinks, our village is calm as a millpond."

"What was his problem yesterday anyway?"

"Lake litter."

"Sounds catchy," said Olivia as she headed back to the incident room. "Lake litter. Be a good name for a band. I like it."

"Direberry surely doesn't. He's complaining about outsiders throwing trash in our lake. Wants the villagers to set up twenty-four-hour surveillance---on a volunteer basis. I told him flat that he can take the first shift and let us know how it goes. Lake litter! Crazy."

"If it's happening, though, we need to get to the bottom of it. Not good for the fish. For once I agree with Chesley, though not about volunteer surveillance. I'll speak with him tonight."

"No, you focus on the murder. Direberry owns half the land around the lake. He can sort it out on his own if it's that important to him. Don't think I won't tell him so myself!"

"I would never bet against you, Ava. Alright, then, I'll just…" Arlen looked around, then hesitated.

Ava put her hands on her hips. "Your coffee and breakfast are in the incident room. I know for a fact you didn't think to fix yourself something at home. You need a keeper! Now, go on and eat before killers and ragtag whozits start traipsing in here."

"I'll gladly follow that order," said Arlen.

"I swanny," she muttered as she went back to arranging the makeshift interview room.

To Arlen's relief, and Rose's barely concealed dismay, Mr. May came willingly---almost cheerfully---into the station.

He wore a pair of olive slacks and a cream button-down shirt under a cashmere coat. A matching beret brought the entire outfit together. His walk was oddly chipper.

"Five bucks says I can make this shot," he said. He looked at Rose expectantly, but she glared back. Undeterred, he turned and tossed his beret. It landed on the coat hook.

"Ha! Lucky you didn't take that bet." He grinned and Arlen looked at him quizzically.

"Mr. May, do you understand why you're here?"

He sobered his expression and bowed his head.

"Yes, I do. I'll save you some time, Chief Well. Not sure how you found out, but I admit everything. I had no choice, you see."

Rose slapped her handcuffs on the table, leaned back in her chair, and smiled broadly. Arlen frowned. "Mr. May, before you say anything, I must caution you---"

"Yes, yes, I understand my rights. Stay silent…used against me…attorney, blah blah blah. I waive all that."

"We'll observe the formalities if you don't mind. Please don't say another word until you've read and signed the waiver that Officer Tern hands you."

Rose drew a paper from a manila folder. "Read it carefully, Mr. May, and let us know if you want an attorney present before we proceed to prosecute you to the fullest extent of the law. This interview is being recorded."

Mr. May carelessly affixed his signature to the waiver. "It looks to be in order. Frankly, it's a relief to talk to you."

Arlen took the paper from Rose. "Mr. May, thank you for your cooperation. I have a few preliminary questions."

"Shoot."

Arlen raised his eyebrows. "First question is why."

"Money, of course. It's always money. Suffered a losing streak and my wife wouldn't hear of covering my debts. Her assets are sacrosanct, you see. The gun was packed in a trunk, doing no one any good. Seemed the logical solution. Needs must and all that."

He giggled shrilly. "Is that a fridge I hear back there? Can I have some water? Or a whiskey?"

He jumped from his chair and headed towards the bamboo screen.

In one fluid motion, Rose stood and pulled her service weapon. "Freeze, Mr. May!"

Mr. May stared agog at Rose. "What are you---?"

Arlen glared at Rose, then steered the flabbergasted man back to his seat. "Don't make sudden moves like that again, Mr. May. For everyone's safety."

"You gave me a heart attack!" sputtered Mr. May. "I know this is a dry village, but can't a man joke about a drink? Is that a crime? My goodness!"

Rose holstered her gun and growled through gritted teeth. "If you want something, ask! I'll get you water."

"If it's no trouble," he replied in a shaky voice. Arlen noticed spots of color on the man's cheeks and a shimmer of sweat around his forehead. Rose thrust a cold bottle of water at him, and he guzzled half of it in one gulp.

"Mr. May, let's continue," said Arlen. "Tell us what you did yesterday, starting from when you woke up."

Mr. May shot Rose a glance, then turned his full attention to Arlen. "I got up around six, did my workout, showered, dressed, and went down for breakfast. Southwestern omelet, three eggs---delicious. Then, I received a call from my friend who..."

Mr. May paused and looked away.

"Who what?"

"Doesn't matter. Anyway, after my wife left, I decided to check out some trunks in the attic. Found an old gun. Took it, did what I did, then came home for lunch. The cook always leaves me something to heat up. Spinach mushroom quiche---scrumptious."

"Mr. May," said Arlen. "I need you to be specific when you say you did what you did."

Mr. May squirmed. "On second thought, I'd rather not. I feel I was well within my rights. Most husbands would agree."

"Are you serious?" Rose exploded.

"Officer Tern---"

"No! Of all the misogynistic, abusive---"

"Hey!" protested Mr. May. "Why are you shouting at me? That's so mean."

"Officer Tern! Observe in silence or send in another officer. Your choice."

Rose settled back in her chair, her face flush.

Arlen resumed. "Mr. May, I'm going to ask a series of questions and you will answer them clearly and concisely. No interruptions, no distractions, no vague generalizations. Do you understand?"

"I'm slightly offended, but yes, I understand."

"Good. You said earlier that you took a gun. Did you use that gun to shoot your wife?"

"What? Heavens, no! Absolutely not."

"Did you use a different gun to shoot your wife?"

"I didn't shoot her at all. That's crazy."

"Earlier you said you admitted to everything. What were you talking about? What did you do with the gun?"

"I was confessing to a different crime---well, not a crime really. More of a transgression. It's marital property after all."

"What is?"

"The gun. I took the gun---Niralya's father's precious antique gun---which was doing no one any good tucked up in the attic--- and sold it to pay my gambling debt. It was more valuable than I thought. Squared me with my friend."

"Yesterday when we arrived at your house, you panicked when you first saw us. Why was that?"

"I thought Niralya found out I took the gun and reported me for theft. Per the terms of the prenup, which she recited to me daily---from memory---everything she inherited from her family was hers and hers alone. Off limits to me. It would be just like her to pretend to press charges to teach me a lesson. She loves her little joke. Loved."

Mr. May stared at the bamboo screen. Arlen let the silence linger for a minute. Mr. May roused himself from his reverie and cleared his throat.

"Anyway, my friend called and wanted his money, like immediately or else. I took the gun to the city to an exclusive shop. They deal with collectors and are very discreet."

"You've done this before."

Mr. May hesitated. "A few times. Emergencies only, you understand, and with dusty old things from the attic. Niralya never went up there. How was she to know?"

"You drove to the city, sold the gun to a dealer, paid your debt, then drove all the way back. Does that sum it up?"

"Perfectly. As I told you, Tuesday is Niralya's day to collect rent and spend the afternoon with Wandalene. I'm left to my own devices. It's my favorite day."

"Mr. May, if you would write down the names and addresses of your friend and the dealer, please. We'll need a full written statement from you later. For now, I'll leave you to your, uh, grief."

Rose shoved a notepad and pen in front of Mr. May. He shook his head. "They wouldn't want me to give the police their information. As I said, they are discreet."

Rose scoffed. "So, they'd rather you were tried for murder---a capital offense, mind you---than help us verify your alibi? Some friends!"

Mr. May grabbed the pen, scribbled the information on the note pad, then handed it to Arlen.

"Thank you, Mr. May. Do not contact them until we give you permission. Do you understand?"

Mr. May lowered his eyes and pursed his lips.

"We'll know if you do," smirked Rose. "From the phone records."

His face paled, but he nodded his head. He looked at Arlen. "What do I do now?"

"I suggest you contact Pastor Deighton and take care of the funeral arrangements."

"That won't take long. Niralya gave him a list of her requirements."

"Requirements?"

"She planned her funeral in advance years ago. Mine, too,

come to think of it. She just had to control everything, didn't she?"

"I think that's very…prudent. I should probably do the same."

Mr. May snorted. "I told her it was bad luck and she ridiculed me. Guess I have the last laugh!"

"Apparently. Shall I drive you home?"

"I expect Nova is waiting to take me."

"Nova Green?"

"Yes. She brought a breakfast casserole this morning while your officer was fetching me. Clucked around like a mother hen. She doesn't understand we have staff for that. Sorry to say our housekeeper took umbrage. Felt it was an insult to her management skills. High words were exchanged before I stepped in. To make Nova feel better, I accepted her kind offer of a lift home when we're finished here."

"I see."

Arlen, Rose, and Ava watched through the front window of the station as Nova Green bustled Mr. May into her car and drove off.

"She is a bit like a mother hen, isn't she?" Arlen observed.

"More like a vulture hen," said Rose. "I expect she and a dozen other women in the village will smother Mr. May with kindness over the coming weeks."

Ava harrumphed. "It's unseemly. Wait until she's buried and prayed over, why don't you? I thought better of Nova, even if she is a newcomer."

"She's been here a good many years," said Arlen. "Sews and crafts, doesn't she?"

"I bought a quilt from her at Christmas," said Rose. "Her stitching is the best I've ever seen. I love that quilt."

"Yes," said Ava. "She's skilled with a needle, I'll give her that. Never took her to be man-crazy, but you never know, do you?"

Arlen shook his head. "Humans are a mystery. I prefer fish."

40

Later that afternoon, the team reassembled in the incident room to confer and update the crime board. Truly and Gavyn had driven into the city to verify Mr. May's alibi. Meanwhile, Rose and Olivia obtained Mrs. May's phone and financial records, and Arlen hounded Dr. Concord for preliminary autopsy findings.

Ava circled the table placing half-moon fried apple pies on blue and white patterned dessert plates. Pitchers of fresh-squeezed lemonade and iced tea sat on a rolling cart and the team helped themselves before getting down to business.

"We'll start with Truly and Gavyn's report," said Arlen.

Truly waved to Gavyn. The young carpenter reddened slightly but stood up at the whiteboard. "Mr. May was at the dealers by nine o'clock when they opened. He sold them an antique pocket revolver for $150,000---"

"Say what?" Rose's jaw dropped.

"Yeah, but he got fleeced," said Gavyn. "I checked the web. A similar piece sold at auction for over one million last year. If he had shopped around, he would have gotten much more."

Arlen's eyes widened. "Perhaps Mrs. May was right to keep him on a tight financial leash."

"Definitely," agreed Truly. "He has a mean gambling habit. His friend---and trust me, that guy's no one's friend---said he runs up tens of thousands of dollars in losses every week. They let him win a little sometimes to keep him coming back. That right there tells me the games are rigged. He was reluctant to talk to me at first, but I told him I have no interest in his business nor do I have jurisdiction in his county. Couldn't shut him up after that. He confirmed that Mr. May paid him ninety grand in cash around ten o'clock yesterday morning, then promptly lost forty grand more. Left around noon, happy as a lark."

"I can't even comprehend these numbers," said Rose. "Who throws that kind of money away each and every week?"

"It boggles the mind," said Arlen. "Too bad you promised not to break up his operation."

"I promised nothing of the sort," said Truly.

He winked at Gavyn who grinned from ear to ear. "Cashel only told him *we* don't have jurisdiction. We didn't promise we wouldn't pass the information on to the law enforcement agency that does."

"Well done," chuckled Arlen. "Rose? Olivia?"

"I'll go first," said Olivia. "From what I saw so far, Mrs. May's financials---I'm still waiting for more reports to come in---are as neat and meticulous as the rest of her life. No debts or liabilities---"

"Unless you count her husband," snorted Rose.

Olivia grinned and continued. "Prudent investments, paid her taxes, maintained her rental properties regularly. She may have been a stickler for the weekly rent, but she was quick to fix anything that broke and she honored the terms of her family's long-term leases. Never once raised the rent since she took over."

"What about Lincoln Zader's lease?" asked Arlen. "She was making a major change there."

"I didn't find anything yet as to why," said Olivia. "We sent a written request to her lawyer in the city. As for the phone records, Rose, why don't you tell them what we found?"

"It's interesting. In addition to her fancy cell phone, that she rarely used, she had three landlines in her home. One was for the household staff to use to order supplies and such. The other was a main house line. Most of the calls in the past month were to or from her few friends in the village. The third line is set up in her private study or home office. The calls on it---except for one---were to her lawyer or to her investment advisor in the city."

"And the exception?" asked Arlen.

"She received a call at 6:00 a.m. on the day she was murdered," said Rose. "Lasted two minutes."

"From?" asked Arlen.

"Her best friend," said Rose. "Wandalene Brackett."

Ava gasped. "You said she acted like she hadn't heard from Niralya since Sunday."

"That's what she implied," agreed Arlen. "She seemed genuinely shocked when we told her about the death. I can't imagine she had anything to do with it."

"Maybe she was shocked that we found the body so quickly," said Truly. "Got upset that she might be found out. If she was the killer, that is. One phone call isn't exactly definitive evidence."

"That's right," agreed Arlen. "But since the call was made shortly before the murder, it's reasonable for us to want to know what was said in case it shines a light on her intentions for the day. We'll need to talk with her, but let's dig a little into her background first. Olivia---"

"I'm on it," said Olivia as she tapped away at her laptop.

Arlen glanced at his watch. "Save it for later. It's time for the village meeting. I don't have to tell you to watch the crowd, listen for anything interesting, and don't give any information away."

"You don't have to tell us, but you did anyway," said Rose. "Don't worry, Chief. What we lack in experience we'll make up for in obedience. For a change."

"Speak for yourself," muttered Ava.

Arlen envisioned a somber, orderly village meeting with the fine, upstanding citizens eager to help their beloved peace officers quickly solve such a shocking case. The culprit would be identified and apprehended, and the village would parade into next week's Winter Festival with the satisfaction that justice had been served and harmony restored to their idyllic community. His vision and reality collided barely five minutes after he hit the gavel to call the meeting to order. To their credit, the villagers allowed him to complete two sentences before the meeting descended into chaos.

"On Tuesday morning, Mrs. Niralya May was found murdered on the road west of the lake. If anyone in the village has information that would be relevant to our investigation, please come forward as soon as possible. We would---"

"What I'd like to know," interrupted Mayor Hutton. "Is what are you doing to protect the rest of us? Are we to sit back and be murdered in our beds?"

"She wasn't murdered in her bed," scoffed his wife. "Unless she took up camping on the west road, which Princess May---I mean, dear Niralya---would not likely do. Be sensible, Riggs!"

Mayor Hutton looked like he wanted to argue with his wife, but he smiled tightly and patted her hand. Arlen tried again. "We would---"

Councilman Direberry stood up. "The big question is how much is this costing the village? Are all these officers on overtime?"

Arlen sighed. "If my officers work overtime to catch a murderer, then they'll be paid overtime in accordance with their contracts. Unless you'd rather we just let this killer go so we can save a few dollars, Chesley."

A few of the villagers booed.

Direberry blustered. "I'm not saying that. But we need to keep an eye on costs. That's all."

"We're mindful of our duties and responsibilities to the village, Chesley. I defy you to find a better team in the whole state than what we're blessed with." Arlen managed to keep his anger under control, but just barely.

"Keep quiet, Brother," said Giddy Hutton. "Chief Well knows what he's doing. Although I'd be obliged if y'all wouldn't let this interfere with my Winter Festival."

"We'll do our best, Miss Giddy." Like Mayor Hutton, Arlen found out long ago that it was best not to cross Giddy Hutton when it came to festivals.

She nodded her head majestically and Arlen continued. "We would---"

"First things first," said Nova Green, jumping from her seat.

44

"We need to set up a rota for family meals. I know what Dax likes. I'll take the first week---"

This was met with a chorus of protests from several women, but before Arlen could restore order a loud, clear voice rang out.

"Excuse me, please! I may be heard, no?"

Arlen watched a tall, muscular woman clothed in a severely cut black suit stand and face the villagers. Her blonde hair was pulled back into a tight bun that rested on the nape of her neck. Her accent was possibly eastern European, but he wasn't sure. He couldn't recall ever seeing her in the village and his curiosity was piqued.

"I am housekeeper for May family," said the woman. She bowed slightly from the shoulder and continued. "I tell you one thing. You have custom---charming custom, I'm sure---to share food with death family. Thank you, not for us. I have menu planned for months. Keep your dishes or give to poor. Good-bye."

She bowed again and turned to leave, but Ms. Green and several women rushed forward to block her exit.

"I'm sure you don't speak for Dax---Mr. May to you," said Ms. Green. Arlen detected a bit of venom in the otherwise honeyed tone. "We're neighbors after all, and just want to express our sympathies to console the bereaved."

"Do at funeral," said the woman. "Stay away from house. As I tell you many times, we don't need you."

With that blunt pronouncement she pushed her way past a stunned Ms. Green. Arlen raised his eyebrows to Rose who hurried after the housekeeper.

Another chorus of exclamations and more than a few impolite remarks rang out. Arlen banged the gavel to restore order. The villagers returned to their seats and appeared ready to listen. Ms. Green's face looked like thunder.

The meeting proceeded but no new information about Mrs. May or the murder was forthcoming. Arlen turned the agenda over to Ava and Giddy Hutton to discuss the upcoming Winter Festival.

Arlen was disappointed that his persons of interest were not in attendance. Mr. May understandably was excused, but Arlen didn't know why neither Lincoln Zader nor Wandalene Brackett bothered to show. He couldn't recall a time that they missed a festival village meeting, much less a mandatory one. No doubt Miss Giddy would get to the bottom of that, and Arlen made a mental note to find out what excuses they gave.

His reverie was interrupted by Ava's stern voice ringing out across the meeting room. "I'm glad y'all appreciate my fruit cocktail cake, but if the person or persons who loved it so much at Christmas that they took the whole cake---sheet pan and all---would kindly return the pan, then I'll be able to make it for the festival."

Arlen scanned the crowd looking for any sign of guilt. He saw young Timothy and his group of friends laughing in the back row. Timothy stood up when he saw Arlen's frown.

"Tweren't us, Chief Well, I promise! But Miss Ava's cake is the best, so you can't blame a body for temptation, can you?"

"Yeah!" said the boys.

Ava beamed at them. "Tell you what. Y'all come to my house after church on Sunday and I'll teach you how to bake it your-selves. I have a dozen cakes to make for the festival and could use the help. I'll feed you dinner for your troubles."

"Wow!" exclaimed Timothy. "Dinner with Miss Ava! That's a deal, right, fellers?"

"Right!"

The meeting broke up shortly after that. Arlen and his team recapped their impressions of the crowd as they put away the folding chairs and tidied the meeting hall.

"Once the festival is over and I can catch my breath," said Ava. "I'm gone have a talk with some of these man-crazy women.

It's indecent and that ain't no lie! I'll see y'all in the morning. I'm tuckered out!"

Arlen nodded his thanks as Ava left, then turned to his remaining team. "Rose, did you find out anything from the housekeeper?"

Rose shook her head. "Only her name. Elke Lina Manfred. Man, I wish I had half her discipline and a tenth of her style. Did you see that hair bun? Perfection! Oh, and she said the household staff expects to be interviewed tomorrow and will welcome us at eight o'clock sharp."

"That's obliging of her," said Truly. "Are any of the staff suspects?"

"We don't know enough about them yet," admitted Arlen. "Rose, you and Truly interview the staff. Gavyn and I will pay a visit to Mr. Zader. Might as well rule him out sooner rather than later. I don't see him as our shooter, but let's follow procedure."

"Keep an open mind," teased Rose. "But I agree we should check on him. Wonder why he wasn't here tonight?"

"I hope he's not feeling poorly," said Gavyn.

"We'll see," said Arlen. "I know it's late, but let's meet in the incident room and update our findings, such as they are."

"I'll be there as fast as I can," said Rose. "I have to go home first."

"Is everything alright?" asked Arlen.

"Yeah, but I need to fetch Ava's sheet cake pan!" With that, she bolted out the door.

5

THE NEXT MORNING AS ARLEN AND GAVYN WERE ABOUT TO leave the station, Pastor Leet Deighton walked in and asked if he could have a word. Arlen ushered him into the newly appointed interview room. Ava manifested a cup of the pastor's favorite oolong tea seemingly out of thin air.

Arlen held the pastor in high regard. The younger man had been born and raised in the village, only leaving to attend seminary college and to go on mission trips. The village church was established by the founding families as nondenominational Protestant but welcomed visiting orators from other churches and faiths with the caveat that they "talk sense." Under Pastor Deighton's leadership, the village was gently schooled in two basic rules: love God and love your neighbor as yourself. Easy concepts to understand, though Arlen had to admit they were difficult to put into practice.

"What can I do for you, Leet?"

"Arlen, I don't know what to do for the best. I think I do, but I'm not sure. Thought I'd pick your brain." The pastor ran his hands through his thick, brown hair. "Niralya May came to me years ago and gave me specific written instructions on how to conduct her services if anything should happen to her."

"I heard that from Mr. May."

"Yes, well, I had forgotten about it for the most part. I thought it was eccentric at the time, but now that I look at it again, I think it may be downright cruel. Or at the very least, not neighborly."

"What did she want?"

"On the day of her service, she wants me to lock the front church door and admit no one other than her husband, myself, and a pianist—your Miss Hope."

"Burklie is not my Miss Hope," interrupted Arlen. "I don't see why people can't be friends without tongues wagging. I thought better of you, Leet."

"More fool you, then," laughed the pastor. "The point is, she wants me to preach a full funeral service, complete with scripture reading and prearranged hymns, to an audience of one. Beats all I ever heard!"

"The village won't like that," mused Arlen. All life events, births, graduations, marriages, and deaths were village affairs. Moreover, on the first of every month, a party for that month's birthday and anniversary honorees was held in the village hall. No invitations were issued as it was understood that the entire village was welcome to attend. Arlen thought the celebrations to be the highlight of each month.

"That church door hasn't been locked in more than two hundred years!" Pastor Deighton continued. "All are welcome to enter. No one's ever been denied."

"What happens if you disregard her instructions?"

The pastor snorted. "She added a codicil to her will---sent me a copy, she did---stating that the church would receive a very large donation if I adhered to her instructions. I'm talking large enough to carry us for years. But, if I deviate even an inch, we get nothing."

"What are your thoughts?"

"Hang the money! She wants to use her services as one last swipe at her husband or maybe at the village. I'll not be a party to manipulating the Lord's house like that. It's spiteful and wrongheaded."

"There's your answer, then. What's the problem?"

"Mr. May told me he wants to follow his wife's wishes! Said he's been looking forward to sitting in that front pew for a long time and that he plans to enjoy the service. Said he's happy that she valued his privacy. Now I don't know what to do!"

"That is a pickle. I honestly don't know what to tell you."

Pastor Deighton sighed and drained his teacup. As soon as he clinked it on the saucer, Ava came in with a fresh cup and a plate of lemon raspberry muffins.

"They're sugar free," said Ava. "I used that newfangled monkfruit that Dr. Min praises to the heavens. Says he's gonna convert us to healthy if it's the last thing he does. We'll see about that."

"That's broadminded of you to give it a try, Miss Ava," said the pastor as he bit into the muffin. "Delicious!"

"We should ask Ava her opinion on your problem," said Arlen as he tentatively took a bite of the healthy muffin.

"I heard the whole thing," said Ava. "These walls are thin, and your voice is a nice low baritone, Pastor. Carries a bit."

"Thank you."

"Here's what you do. The doctor called and said the body can be released to the family. Have Mr. May's private service on Friday. Lock the front door but keep the side doors unlocked---to ease your conscience. Announce a village-wide service for Saturday and do the burial then. Don't say a peep about Friday. That doesn't go against her wishes, does it?"

Pastor Deighton brightened up. "No, it doesn't. She didn't say anything about the side doors or about having a second service. That's a perfect solution. Thank you, Miss Ava."

Arlen shook his head. "Ava could rule the world if she wasn't so busy baking and keeping us in line around here."

"I swanny." Ava swatted at his arm and bustled out, but Arlen could see the smile on her face.

With the unusual funeral arrangements sorted, Arlen and Gavyn headed to the cottages east of the lake to check on Lincoln Zader. In contrast to the May's mansion, the cottages, which were lined up in a row along the road, were small and plainly built. White picket fences separated each rectangular lot and gave the residents a bit of privacy. The modest front yards were uniformly neat and well maintained. Arlen knew from prior visits that the back yards were larger and dotted with trees and flowering shrubs. A few of the tenants maintained small tabletop vegetable and herb gardens because the ground in this area was too rocky to plant. The chill of winter left everything stark and bare, but in the spring, the loveliness of the flowers and trees transformed the neighborhood into a beautiful sight.

Arlen stepped onto the bare front porch and knocked. The door opened and Lincoln Zader stared warily at Arlen but broke into a smile when he saw Gavyn.

"Boy, you better git in here out da cold," said the old man. "Bring that boss of yours if you have to. 'Spect he's frozen, too."

"Hey, Mr. Lincoln," smiled Gavyn. "Much obliged. It's right cold and no mistake!"

Arlen and Gavyn followed Mr. Zader into his cozy, tidy sitting room. Arlen shut the front door behind him and carefully stepped around a white quartz doorstop the size of a football. He noticed a .22-gauge rifle in a vertical frame on the wall by the door. This was not unusual in the country, but Arlen made a mental note to check the weapon before they left.

"Good of you to see us, Mr. Zader," said Arlen as they sat down.

"You're here about my landlady, I 'spect."

"That's right. We have a few questions, if you don't mind."

"And if I do mind, you'll ask them anyway, won't you?" The old man cackled.

Arlen smiled. "That we will, but we'd rather have a friendly talk. See if you can help us puzzle this out."

Mr. Zader looked sad. "Knew something was wrong when she didn't show up Tuesday. You could set your watch by that woman, that's how on time she always was. Gotta admire that in today's willy-nilly world."

"She certainly was disciplined," Arlen agreed.

"She was that, absolutely. Not the friendliest sort, if we're honest. Sharp-eyed and all business, that one. Still, she kept these cottages in good shape. Not for our sakes, mind you. If anyone said a word of thanks, she would scoff and say that it's to keep up the value of her investment. Never could figure her out, tell the truth."

"Mr. Lincoln," said Gavyn gently. "We heard you had words with her last week."

Mr. Zader hung his head. "That I did, son. I regret that now, though she got my dander up. Asked me to leave after all these years! Didn't give a reason or any complaint against me. Just out of the blue one day. I admit I saw ten shades of red and I let her know it in no uncertain terms!"

"No one can blame you for being upset," said Arlen. "But, seeing as what happened to Mrs. May, we have to ask you officially if you had anything to do with it. You don't have to talk with us if you don't want to, and you can have an attorney present."

"Sorry, Mr. Lincoln," said Gavyn.

"You're doing your job, son. That's what you're paid for. I don't mind, 'cause I never harmed a hair on that woman's head. Burned her ears up a bit with some home truths, now I admit to that. Nothing more."

Gavyn looked visibly relieved, but Arlen had to press on. "That's good to hear, Mr. Zader. Can you tell us where you were on Tuesday morning and if anyone saw you?"

"I was right here, waiting to pay my rent like everyone else.

Eight o'clock came and went, she didn't show up. That was odd, so I went next door to ask my neighbor if he knew what was what. He didn't have no idea. We had a cup of coffee and waited. She didn't show up, so I went on about my business. Figured we'd hear something soon enough."

"Did anyone see you before eight?"

"Don't know if they did or didn't. I got my own things to worry about."

"Do you have a handgun, Mr. Zader? I saw that nice hunting rifle up front, but do you have a pistol?"

"Naw, sir. I ain't had no use for one. Hunting varmints is all I use that one for, and that's been a while. Check it if you want. Don't make me no nevermind."

Arlen nodded to Gavyn who got up and checked the rifle. "Not loaded and not fired for a while. Needs cleaning, Mr. Lincoln. I can stop by soon and do that for you if you like. Bring Dad with me."

"That'd be a treat, for sure. Your folks are good people."

As Gavyn put the rifle away, Arlen broached the next topic. "Mr. Zader, do you know if your eviction is cancelled now that Mrs. May is deceased?"

"Now that's an interesting story and I don't mind telling you I was flummoxed for a minute or two."

"Why is that?"

"Yesterday me and all the neighbors got a call from a city lawyer about the rent. Said Mrs. May left instructions that if she died, all the tenants would get one month's free rent as a memorial of some sort. I ain't never heard of such a thing, but we appreciate it. Don't mind telling you that free money is one of my favorite things."

He laughed and slapped his knee.

"Can't blame you for that."

"I asked that lawyer feller if I still had to leave and he said he didn't know nothing about it. Told me to carry on like always.

Said these properties belong to the husband now seeing as how it was a wedding present from her folks. It's separate from the rest of the family money."

"That's interesting. I hope Mr. May keeps things the way they are and doesn't raise your rent."

Mr. Zader shifted in his seat. "I wanted to ask him if he had a mind to sell. Me and a couple others have some money set by and could swing it if he don't ask for the moon. Don't know when it would be seemly to bring it up, though, with his grief fresh and all. What do you think?"

Arlen considered. "I think you can mention it after the service on Saturday. See what he says."

Mr. Zader brightened. "That's exactly what I'll do!"

"We'd best be on our way. We still got a killer to catch. Thank you for your time, Mr. Zader." As Arlen stood, he noticed a metal rod sticking out from behind the sofa.

"What you got there, Mr. Zader?"

"That's my new hobby! It's a doozy, too. Magnet fishing."

"What's magnet fishing, Mr. Lincoln?" asked Gavyn.

"Grab that thing, son, and I'll show you."

Gavyn pulled the device out and handed it to the old man. Arlen saw that it was a pole attached to a rope with a small, round one-sided magnet. Mr. Zader opened a drawer and pulled out a handful of nuts and bolts and placed them on the coffee table. He angled the magnet over the items, and they quickly jumped up and attached to the magnet.

Mr. Zader grinned from ear to ear. "That never gets old."

"Looks like fun," agreed Gavyn.

Arlen was puzzled. "I guess I don't see how that helps you catch fish, Mr. Zader."

That brought a hoot of laughter from the old man. "It's not for fish, man. It's to look for metal in the streams and lake. People lose the darndest things. I've found tools, a bevy of fishhooks, and once an old bicycle. Fixed it up for my neighbor's girl to ride."

"That's clever," said Arlen. "You're doing the village a service by cleaning up the waters 'round here. Councilman Direberry has a bee in his bonnet about litter getting thrown in the lake by outsiders."

Mr. Zader shook his head. "Ain't just outsiders. I seen villagers chunk a thing or two in the lake when they think no one's watching."

"You can report them to us, if you want."

"No, you're busy enough with this here killing. I'll have a quiet word with 'em next chance I get. We'll straighten it out, don't you worry."

"That reminds me. You weren't at the festival meeting last night. Is everything okay?"

"I told Miss Giddy I had someplace to be, and she wouldn't hear of it. Now, I don't like talking back to a young lady, but I also don't like being bossed around. Told her if she don't like it, she can git somebody else to mind the Odds 'n Ins table. I've done it for nigh on forty years and if I ain't earned a rest from one meeting, I don't know who has!"

"Can't argue with you there. Thank you again, Mr. Zader. We'll see ourselves out."

As they drove back to the station, Arlen mulled over the meager facts of the case as Gavyn read his notes.

"Chief, what do we do next? Should we talk with Ms. Brackett?"

"That's exactly what we should do, Gavyn. Thank you for reminding me."

The young carpenter blushed and went back to his notes.

Wandalene did not look pleased to see them, but she invited them in and sat down.

"Thank you for your time, Ms. Brackett," said Arlen. "We missed you at the meeting last night."

Wandalene raised her eyebrows. "If that Hutton woman set the law on me because I didn't adhere to her mandatory meeting schedule, then you tell her from me that she better watch her step. I'll move to the city, I will, and her blasted festival can carry on without me!"

"Miss Giddy didn't send us, Ms. Brackett. We just want to ask you a few questions with the idea that you might help us find your friend's killer."

Ms. Brackett's eyes misted up. "I'm sorry, Chief Well. I didn't go last night because I am not up to facing a crowd. I can't focus on how many jars of blackberry jam we plan to sell when Niralya is in the---the morgue."

The tears spilled over, but she swiped them away.

Arlen nodded and Gavyn looked down at the floor. "We're sorry for your loss, Ms. Brackett. We understand that you and Mrs. May were at school together. That's a long friendship, something to be treasured."

"You're right, she was a treasure. Oh, I don't mean she was perfect. She had her quirks like everyone else. But we usually saw eye to eye on most things. Except that man, of course."

"That man?"

"Her husband. He's the one you should be talking to. No doubt in my mind that he shot her! Ask him where he was that day, and you'll see."

"We did ask him. I can't go into details, but I can tell you that we confirmed that Mr. May was not in the village at the time Mrs. May was shot. He was in the city. We have two witnesses."

Wandalene shook her head. "That's as may be, but I tell you he's behind it. He didn't give two hoots for Niralya. Loved her money and their lifestyle; didn't love her. I don't know what possessed her to marry him. She knew what he was, but because he was what some women would consider handsome, she overlooked his flaws. Made me sick."

"Is that what you argued with her about Sunday night?"

56

Wandalene hesitated. "Yes. I asked her point blank why she didn't get rid of him. She felt insulted and blasted me with a little more heat than I thought she would. My mistake, of course. I planned to apologize at lunch on Tuesday. But…I never got the chance."

"Is that why you called her at six a.m. that morning? To apologize?"

Wandalene looked confused. "What are you talking about? I may live in the sticks, but I keep late hours. I sleep until eight o'clock. I didn't call her."

6

ARLEN STARED AT THE CEILING OF THE INCIDENT ROOM AND TRIED to make sense out of what they had learned that day. Gavyn updated the whiteboard but turned the marker over to Truly when he and Rose returned from interviewing the May's household staff. Olivia sat at the end of the table engrossed in the screen of her laptop.

Ava bustled in and cleared the table of empty cups and glasses. "Y'all need to wash your hands and come out front to have some dinner while the food is hot. It's a spread fit for a king, all courtesy of Burklie and Ana Sofia. Who, by the way, are waiting to say hey to their menfolk."

Arlen took exception to being called anyone's menfolk, but he didn't argue because he was hungrier than he wanted to admit. He quickly washed his hands and then filed into the main station room behind his team. He stopped short at the door. The station had been transformed to resemble a little café with folding card tables complete with linen tablecloths, placemats, and votive candles in the center.

"What in the world?"

Burklie Hope, the village church piano player and music teacher, smiled broadly. "Not my fault, I promise! If it was up to me, I'd throw you a chicken wing and tell you to get back to work. This is all Ava's doing. Ain't she something?"

Arlen gave Burklie a side hug and nodded his head. "That she is."

"Make a plate, Chief Well," said Ana Sofia. "Before everything gets cold. You and Cashel need energy to catch this killer. Which I know you can't talk about, so that's all I'll say about that!"

"Thank you for understanding, Ana Sofia," smiled Arlen. "It's nothing personal. We're just following procedure."

"They know that," said Ava as she put lace coasters by their plates. "Now eat up and let's finish this case and get back to normal."

"Yes, ma'am," said Arlen. He sat down to enjoy the meal and hadn't taken two bites when Giddy Hutton burst in and stood looking shocked at the scene before her.

"What in the world?" she exclaimed.

"That's what I said, too, Miss Giddy," said Arlen. "Burklie and Ana Sofia made dinner for us, and Ava decided we'd eat in style."

"There's plenty, Hon," said Ava. "We'd love for you to join us."

Arlen's conscience pricked a little because in truth he wouldn't love that. Still, he backed up Ava's invitation with as much warmth as he could muster.

"Thank you, but I've got dinner waiting for me at home," said Giddy. "I came by to ask if y'all would help collect stuff for the Odds 'n Ends table. Old Lincoln Zader will man the table, but he's not up to running around picking stuff up."

"Miss Giddy, we'd love to help," Arlen lied. "But as you know, we're focused on Mrs. May's murder right now."

"Are you sure it's a murder, though?" asked Giddy. "Like...as not it was an accident. I mean, what evidence do you really have that it was murder?"

She looked from one person to the other, and Arlen noted she was frowning in that way she had when someone crossed her or interfered with her festival doings.

"Miss Giddy, thank you for your input," said Arlen carefully. "We'll take what you said into consideration. In the meantime---"

"It wouldn't be out of your way," Giddy insisted. "You're probably running around talking to people anyway. I don't see why you can't collect a few things while you're out and about."

"You want us to collect odds and ends from potential suspects while we're on duty?" asked Rose. "Use it like a ruse to get in their houses?"

"Well...."

"I volunteer!" said Rose. "That's brilliant, Miss Giddy. You'd make a fine detective."

"I don't know about that," Giddy blushed. "Just trying to get this festival to run as smooth as usual despite these unexpected circumstances."

Arlen shook his head. "No, Rose. I need you to focus on your job. I'm sure there's other villagers who would love to take on this task."

Giddy handed Arlen a sheet of paper. "If you find any, give them this list. I need the items in the town hall by Saturday noon. Sharp!"

With that pronouncement, she sailed out the door. Arlen stood with his mouth open, then glared at his team when they burst into laughter.

"I'm not sure y'all appreciate the seriousness of a murder investigation," he said. "We have a job to do!"

"Here, give me the list," said Burklie. "I don't mind picking up a few things."

"I'll help you," offered Ana Sofia.

"Chief, I don't know if we should send them out there alone," said Truly. "There's still a killer on the loose. What if it's one of the people on this list?"

Burklie dropped the paper like a hot potato. "I hadn't thought about that. Now I'm nervous."

"I'll protect you, Miss Burklie," laughed Ana Sofia. "I'm strong. Ask Cashel. I beat him at arm wrestling last Sunday."

Truly nodded. "That she did. Whether it was fair and square is still open for debate. Still, I'm uneasy about this. Some of these farms are way out in the county and cell service can be spotty."

Gavyn and Olivia had been quiet throughout the entire episode and Arlen saw them exchange a glance.

"What is it, Gavyn?"

"Someone should go with them. Just to be safe."

Arlen pinched his nose, then rubbed his temples. "Rose---"

"Hot dog!" Rose exclaimed. "Gobble your food, ladies! We've got work to do."

After dinner, Arlen and the remaining members of his team went back to the incident room.

"Olivia, are you sure---"

"Yes. The call to Mrs. May came from Ms. Brackett's landline."

"She said she wasn't even awake yet," said Gavyn.

"If she's telling the truth---and it seemed to me that she was," said Arlen. "Then someone else, presumably our killer, went into her house and placed the call."

"She couldn't be sure that she locked her doors," said Gavyn. "Some folks don't around here, so that's not unusual."

"Gavyn didn't find any prints on her phone or the handle of the back door," said Truly. "Ms. Brackett's should have been on there, but they were wiped clean. I think you're right, Chief. The killer took steps to make it look like Ms. Brackett made that call."

"Agreed," said Arlen. "They either wanted to throw suspicion at Ms. Brackett or just waste our time. Which they did. Any chance it had something to do with Mr. May's so-called gambling friend?"

"I don't think so," said Truly. "That guy runs a small, albeit profitable, operation. From what we found, all of his crew were there when Mr. May paid off his debt. They could be lying, of course, but since he was able to come up with the money every week, they had no reason to hurt Mrs. May."

Arlen nodded. "What about the household staff?"

"For some reason, they all love Rose," said Truly. "Even that Elke woman warmed up to her."

"Did Rose show her disdain of Mr. May?"

"She was professional, but yeah, it came through loud and clear," admitted Truly. "I don't think any of them like him. They appeared loyal to Mrs. May, though, so I don't see any motive they would have for killing her."

"Olivia and I followed up on their alibis, Chief," said Gavyn. "They were in the city. We have video from the shops they visited that morning. They're in the clear."

Arlen stared at the whiteboard. "Seems like everyone is in the clear, doesn't it? What are we missing?"

Ava knocked on the open door. "Wandalene Brackett is here and wants to talk to you. I put her in the interview room."

Arlen pointed to Truly. "You come with me. Gavyn, you and Olivia man the equipment and observe."

"Yes, sir."

In the interview room, Arlen thanked Wandalene for coming in and let her know that the interview would be recorded.

"That's fine, Chief Well," she said. "I need to talk to somebody. This is tearing me up since we last spoke."

"I understand," said Arlen. "Now, what would you like us to know?"

"I want to leave," Wandalene said. "I can't stand the thought of someone coming in my house while I was sleeping. There's no reason for me to stay anyway now that Niralya's gone. I only came here for her sake."

"I see," said Arlen. "No one can blame you for how you feel,

Ms. Brackett. It'd be a loss to the village seeing as how you always do so much at the festivals, but I understand."

Wandalene snorted. "That Hutton woman and her pack can get along just fine without me, I assure you. I only helped as a favor to Niralya. She found the festivals quaint and charming, but then she always pawned the real work off on me or her staff. That Nova Green, and some of the others that hang onto Dax's every word, will be more than happy to take my place."

She looked down at her hands and tugged at the hem of her sweater. Arlen and Truly exchanged a glance.

"Is there something more, Ms. Brackett?" asked Truly.

She looked from him to Arlen. "He did it. I don't know how, but I know he killed her."

"Who did, Ms. Brackett?"

"That man. Dax!" she spat. "Everything handed to him on a plate, but he always wanted more. You need to arrest him!"

"I'm sorry, Ms. Brackett," said Arlen. "I can't discuss the case details, but we checked Mr. May's alibi and he was in the city that morning. That's been confirmed."

"Doing what, I'd like to know! Probably with one of his ladies. Niralya was a fool."

Arlen hesitated. "I don't know about that. But, in general terms, he sold an item of value and then paid a debt. He wasn't in the village at the time Mrs. May was shot. I hope that puts your mind at rest."

Wandalene frowned and tilted her head. "Why would he need to sell anything?"

"Mrs. May wouldn't advance the funds he needed, so he sold an item."

"I'm confused. Why didn't he use his own money?"

"Apparently he didn't have any."

"That's impossible. Three weeks ago, he won a prize in the state lottery. Even after taxes, he would have had a bundle. I told

Niralya I saw it on the lottery website---I play occasionally. She planned to claim half of it, per the terms of her prenup."

"I suppose he spent it."

"How could anyone spend three million dollars in three weeks?"

7

DAXTON MAY SQUIRMED IN HIS CHAIR IN THE INTERVIEW ROOM. "You're going to make me late for the funeral."

"The church is a short walk away," said Arlen. "We'll have you out in plenty of time. We need to clarify a few things."

Mr. May looked at his watch and nodded.

"Tell us about the lottery winnings."

"How did you—? Oh, never mind. Yes, I won a packet on the lottery. Not that it matters now."

"What happened?"

"It was a nice amount…three million, but taxes ate half of it. After Niralya's cut, per the blasted prenup, it wasn't really enough."

"Enough for what?"

"To leave, at least for a while. She was the most controlling woman I've ever known. I was fed up. Divorce was out of the question, but I thought if I had a beefy nest egg, I could at least run away for a while. Of course, if it didn't work out, she'd take me back."

"How much did you think you needed?"

"At least a couple of million. Separate from my gaming

money, of course. But, after taxes and Niralya's portion, I had less than one million. Unacceptable."

"What did you do?"

Mr. May looked away and pursed his lips. "I thought if I doubled it, I could take off for Europe for a while. South of France, or Italy. Lots of parties and events coming up. It would have been fun."

"You weren't able to double it, I take it."

"No. Had a bit of bad luck. Problem is I trusted an out-of-state game---I thought I understood it but...live and learn. Lost the bundle."

"Did you tell Mrs. May about this?"

"I told no one. I'm still reeling from it, to be honest. Tried to figure a way to recoup my losses. See, I lost Niralya's share, too. Thank God she died before she found out, or it would be my murder you'd be investigating!"

"That was fortunate for you indeed."

Mr. May had the good graces to blush. "I'm sorry. It sounds bad, but I'm just being honest with you, Chief Well. My marriage was miserable, and I don't see any point in pretending. Now, if there's nothing else, I have a service to attend."

Arlen waved at him to leave. He went back to the incident room and found his entire team assembled.

"Wow, just wow," said Rose. "That guy is a piece of work."

"I'm glad I'm poor," said Truly. "No one would be with me for the money."

"Me, either," chimed Gavyn and Olivia.

Arlen stared at the whiteboard and tapped his pencil on the table. Ava poked her head in the door. "Judge Tanner is here. Where do you want to meet with her?"

"The new interview room is fine. Truly is with me. Rose, you and Olivia continue to go through the financials. Ask Ana Sofia to help, if you need to. Gavyn, pick up where Olivia left off with background checks on everyone. There's something we're missing."

The team nodded their agreement and got to work. Arlen was happy to see Judge Xael Tanner. Originally from the city, after she was appointed as a magistrate for the district, she bought a small cottage near the village square. Her itinerary took her to many of the county's small towns and villages. She was smart, practical, and well-respected. Arlen had no doubt that someday she would be elected as a district judge, if she chose to run.

Arlen shook her hand. "Thank you for coming on short notice."

"Not a problem. I planned to be in the area anyway. Hey, Cashel. Did you get my message about being available for weddings?"

"Ha-ha," said Truly dryly. "Just so you know, if I ever get married, it will be in the church. You'll be invited, of course. But that's a big if, so don't buy a hat just yet."

Judge Tanner smiled. "I'm sorry for teasing you. I just think y'all are the cutest couple. Not my business, though, and I promise I'll stay out of it. Well…I'll try."

The two grinned at each other and Arlen shook his head. "We appreciate how quickly you processed the search warrants for the May case. Are you here to talk about that?"

"No, I've done all I can do for you until more evidence comes to light. I'm here to pick your brain for a change."

"It's slim pickings, but I'll help you if I can."

"I like this village, which as you know is why I bought a little cottage here. But I may have to rethink my situation if industry moves in."

Arlen frowned. "What industry do you mean?"

"Mining. Not that I'm against progress in general, but it would mean an influx of workers, trucks tearing up the roads, and a slew of environmental issues. That's not what I was looking for when I sought out a quiet country cottage."

"Mining?" asked Truly. "I haven't heard anything about that. Have you, Chief?"

Arlen shook his head. "Where did you hear this from?"

Judge Tanner looked down. "I'm embarrassed to say that I flat out eavesdropped one day at the records office in the city. I heard someone talking about mineral rights and the legalities of extracting ore. It was interesting at first, then I heard them say it was near Hutton Village and my jaw dropped."

"Do you know who it was or where exactly they were talking about?"

"No. It was an older man---I mean very old, like past eighty. He said something about it being in the east. That's all I know."

"Sounds like Mr. Zader," said Truly.

Arlen nodded. "That it does. It could explain his newfound interest in metal fishing."

"Metal fishing? What in the world is that?" asked Judge Tanner.

As Arlen explained it, he felt more and more uneasy. "When did you hear this conversation in the city?"

"Tuesday morning, about eleven thirty."

Truly looked puzzled. "Didn't he say he was with his neighbors?"

Arlen frowned. "He did, but in truth, I didn't get a firm time-line. That's my fault. I'll go back and talk to him. Truly, you stay here and help the team."

"Right, Chief."

"Judge Tanner, I'll give you a call when I get to the bottom of this. Thanks for the heads up."

Judge Tanner nodded.

As Arlen drove to the eastern cottages, he replayed his prior interview with Mr. Zader in his head. He mentally kicked himself for not pressing for a detailed timeline. As much as he liked the old man, Mr. Zader had plenty of time to shoot Mrs. May and make it home by eight o'clock to be seen by his neighbors. If the mineral rights issue pertained to his cottage, then that would add to his possible motive. *I hope I'm wrong.*

Mr. Zader gave Arlen a sour look but beckoned him to come into the house. "Figured you'd be back. Wish you'd brought the boy. I got a cabinet for him to look at. Needs fixing."

"I'll let Gavyn know, Mr. Zader. First, though, I want you to tell me again what you did on Tuesday morning from the time you woke up."

"Why? It's my business what I do of a day. Nothing to interest you."

"Your landlady was murdered that day so everything pertaining to her interests me."

"That's got nothing to do with me. My neighbors will tell you I was right here, so that's the end of that. See yourself out."

Arlen didn't move from his chair. He stared at the old man until Mr. Zader squirmed and looked away. "If you must know, I got up at five o'clock, like usual, and did a little metal fishing in the lake. Came home, made breakfast, and waited for the lady to git the rent. She didn't show up and the neighbors and all couldn't figure it out. Then, I went to the city. I never laid eyes on her that day. End of story."

"Where exactly did you fish at in the lake?"

"I headed to the south shore near Possum Pier about six something, not sure the exact time. It was cold as a frosted frog, let me tell you. Took my little rowboat and fished the edges where folks like to throw things. Didn't get much…just a few fishhooks. It was almost sunrise, so I figured I'd better head home and wait to pay my rent."

"Did anyone see you when you were out on the lake?"

"No. I seen a lady on the pier as I was rowing around the bend. Don't know if she saw me."

"Who was it?"

"I thought it was one of them newcomers, but it was still a

might dark. She threw something off the pier and was gone by the time I reached the shore."

"Are you sure it was a woman?"

"Seemed like it from the build and the coat. Had a scarf over her hair. Light color. That's how I spotted her in the first place."

"Did you try to find what it was she threw away?"

"No, I didn't have time if I was to get home before eight to meet my landlady."

"Why do you say it was a newcomer?"

"Newcomer, outsider, I don't know. I didn't' recognize 'em. I could be wrong."

"Would you be willing to let us use your magnet to see if we can find what she threw away?"

"What's that got to do with anything?"

"I don't know, but since it happened close to the time of the murder, I think we ought to look into it."

"Fine with me. Send the boy over and I'll show him where to look."

"Thank you. Now, after Mrs. May didn't show up that morning, you went to the city."

Mr. Zader looked at his hands. "I did."

"You went to inquire about mineral rights."

His head shot up. "How the heck do you know that?"

"You were seen and overheard. Do you mind telling me what that's about?"

"That's private business and I'll thank you to not spread that rumor around the village!"

"Mr. Zader, if this has to do with Mrs. May's property, then I need to know about it. Truth be told, that gives you another motive to do away with her, as if the eviction weren't enough. I'm sorry to speak plainly, but I need to get to the bottom of what happened to that poor woman."

Mr. Zader winced. "I didn't hurt her, I swear. I'd never do such a thing no matter how much I need the money."

Arlen softened. "Why do you need money? The village will help, you know."

Mr. Zader shook his head and wiped a tear. "Not for me. My great-granddaughter. She had an operation and they's insurance don't cover it all. I worked out a payment plan with the hospital and I've been scavenging and selling whatever I can to pay it off. My son and his wife do their best, but I love that young 'un too much to not help."

"When did you stumble on the gold? At least I'm assuming it's gold, judging by all the white quartz rocks you have around your house."

"You're a smart one, I'll give you that. Yep, I was digging out some quartz thinking I could sell it to some rock collectors for a few hunnerd. Low and behold I found chunks of gold ore big as your hand. Providence from the Lord, I tell you. I took 'em a few cities away 'cause I didn't want anyone to know. So far, I've paid off half the hospital bill. Not to speak ill of the dead, but I think that landlady of mine figured it out and that's why she wanted to chuck me outta here. Keep the gold for herself."

"That could be."

"I got to wondering if I'd done her wrong by selling the ore, seeing as it's her land and all. That's why I went to the records office and asked them about the mineral rights. They said they's can't give me legal advice, but they read my rental agreement and it don't say a word about minerals. I took that to mean finders keepers."

"But if she were to evict you, that source of funds would be gone."

"That it would, but I'd have to trust the Lord to provide another way. A way that don't include killing nobody!"

"Getting back to the woman on the pier, are you sure you didn't recognize her?"

"No, I was too far away." Suddenly, Mr. Zader snapped his fingers.

"You know what, though? She got in a dark sedan style car. I've seen it around the village, but I don't know the woman's name. Newcomer. Pretty sure she's not married. Always hanging around my landlady at church and festivals and such. Guess they're friends. I'm not a hunnerd percent sure, mind you."

"Thank you, Mr. Zader. Last thing and I promise I'll leave you in peace. Do you have any intention of doing more mining or bringing in work crews? Assuming you have mineral rights like you think?"

"No, sir. I'm keeping this quiet. Once that hospital is paid, I'll be done. Are you going to tell the village?"

Arlen shook his head. "No, that doesn't seem wise. Word will get out and we'll have a gold rush on our hands. That'd be a mess for sure. I promise I'll keep this to myself. Won't even tell my team. So long as you be careful and not let the cat out of the bag."

Mr. Zader cackled. "Don't worry about that. I told a fib, may the Lord forgive me, and told the assayer I traveled three states over and brought it back."

Arlen smiled. "That's good. I'll send Gavyn out to see if y'all can fish out what the woman threw in the lake. It might not be related, but better to check anyway. Thank you for your time."

Mr. Zader hesitated and looked at the floor. "You're welcome back anytime. Seems like you're good people after all. Sorry if I thought different. I don't get on much with the law."

"I understand."

The men shook hands and Arlen left. On the way back to the station, he radioed Gavyn. As he drove south, Arlen decided on a whim to turn into the road that led to Possum Pier. He saw a dark sedan parked a few yards away from the pier. As he drew closer, he saw a woman in a dark coat standing on the pier.

As he approached, he could see the woman's shoulders heaving and heard her plaintive sobs. He walked up quietly.

"Ms. Brackett."

Wandalene twirled around and shock filled her tear-stained

face. She held a medicine bottle that she shoved into her coat pocket.

"I'd prefer to be alone, if you don't mind."

Arlen nodded. "It's a nice spot for it, I'll give you that."

"I don't know what you're talking about."

"When my wife died, I stood on this pier. Looked at the water and thought, why not? What's left for me to live for?"

Wandalene gasped. "What---?"

"Then, suddenly a little swarm of mayflies skated across the lake and this big ole trout jumped out of the water and caught one. That snapped me out of it, and I went on home and cried my eyes out."

"I'm sorry."

"Of course, it was easier for me than it is for you. As a widower, I could grieve openly. Folks understood. You have to keep it bottled up. Hidden."

Wandalene bowed her head.

Arlen continued. "You loved her."

"We loved each other. She was my soulmate. Are you shocked?"

"No. I'm not an expert, but from my experience, love is love. You can't help how you feel. Was there a reason you two couldn't be open?"

Wandalene sniffed. "Her family made it clear when she was younger that they would accept nothing short of a traditional marriage. She gave them Dax. Serves them right, in my opinion."

"Why didn't she divorce him after her parents died?"

"Pride, I think. She still has extended family on the coast, and she keeps in touch with the so-called important people in our social set. She would never admit to failure. Not even for me."

"That's why you argued on Sunday."

Wandalene nodded. "I was fed up. Threatened to move away and be done with her. She laughed and said that's a shame, but she would live."

"Unfortunately, she didn't, did she?"

"No." Wandalene stared out over the lake. "The worst part is that my last words to her were so bitter and hateful. I'll never be able to take that back."

"When I was…at my worst, Dr. Concord found me a grief counsellor in the city. I didn't want to go, but if you know Jackleen, you know she doesn't take no for an answer. Drove me there herself. Took a while, but it eventually helped. The grief never goes away, to be honest. You learn to live with it."

"I don't know if I can do that."

"Will you think about it?"

"Yes. I'll think about it."

Arlen reached out his hand. "Good. Then you won't need that bottle."

Wandalene grimaced but handed over the bottle of pills. Arlen looked at the pale-yellow scarf that she had tied around her hair.

"One more thing, Ms. Brackett. Did you come here Tuesday morning and throw something into the lake?"

"You mean litter? Of course not. I can't stand people who do that. Bad for the environment."

"Remember that the next time you want to throw yourself in the water, would you please? That's the kind of litter I'd have to deal with and I'm busy enough looking for your friend's killer."

Wandalene broke into a laugh. "You are something, Chief Well. But you make a good point. I'll think things through a little better next time. If there is a next time."

"I hope there's not. Let's head back to the village, shall we? Dr. Concord should be in her office. I'll follow your car."

8

ARLEN AND HIS TEAM GATHERED IN THE INCIDENT ROOM. AVA circled the table, placing baked turkey rolls next to muffins on light-blue porcelain plates.

"I got a mess of wild ramps from my sister down south and decided to give y'all a savory snack to go with my black walnut muffins."

"You spoil us, Ava," said Arlen.

"That I do," she muttered as she took her seat.

Arlen stood at the whiteboard. "We'll start without Gavyn. We've learned a few things since we last met, so let's go over the facts once again. Maybe something will jump out at us. Let's start with the husband."

"My money's on him," said Rose. "His alibi witnesses could be lying."

"Yeah, but the video footage from the dealer shows him waiting outside shortly before nine o'clock Tuesday morning," said Truly.

"He could have shot her earlier," argued Rose. "The household staff were out of the house before six o'clock for their day off. We only have his word that Mrs. May left around seven.

We've seen how fast he drives. He could have shot her and made it to the city in record time with that sports car of his."

"Rose makes a good point," said Arlen. "Mr. May also had means considering how many firearms his father-in-law left in the house. There must be a .22 pistol in there somewhere."

Truly nodded. "We searched the house and came upon a few, in addition to the antique guns that old Mr. Brown collected. None of them had been recently fired, however, though he could have tossed the one he used."

"Or sold it," said Rose.

Arlen nodded. "So, he had means. Motive is undeniable. Loveless marriage on top of money issues."

"I'm telling you, he's our guy," said Rose.

"Opportunity is there as well," said Truly. "If we assume he lied about the timeline or that he broke the speed record getting to the city. Or both."

"He could have hired someone," said Rose. "Assuming he could hold on to money long enough to pay them."

"Assumptions are not enough for an arrest warrant," said Arlen. "We need proof. Moving on, our next suspect is old Lincoln Zader. He had a strong motive because of the eviction."

"He's lived in that cottage for over forty years," said Truly. "No doubt he's attached to the place, but is that enough to kill someone over? It's not like he would be homeless. The Pepper family would set him up on their property, right, Olivia?"

"Absolutely. We'd love to have him as a close neighbor. Dad wouldn't even charge him rent."

Ava patted Olivia on the arm. "Your people are good-hearted."

Olivia blushed and turned her focus to her laptop.

Arlen didn't want to mention the gold mining, so he moved on. "Means is tricky. He says he doesn't have a .22 pistol, just a rifle. It hasn't been fired recently. Olivia, do we know if any other guns are registered to him?"

"No. Just the .22 rifle is on file."

"It's possible he has an unregistered gun, but we'll leave that for now. Opportunity?"

"He waited at home for Mrs. May to collect the rent and then spent time with his neighbors," said Truly. "Did he have anything to add when you spoke with him again?"

"Yes," said Arlen as he wrote on the whiteboard. "He went metal fishing in the lake before breakfast. On his way home, he saw a woman throw something in the lake off Possum Pier. Gavyn is out with Mr. Zader now to see if they can retrieve whatever she threw away. Might be nothing, but the timing on the day of the murder means we should at least look."

"Did he see who the woman was?" asked Ava.

"No. Said she had a dark coat, a light head scarf, and drove away in a dark sedan."

"That could be half the women in the village, including me, and no telling how many from the city," said Ava.

"Villagers know better than to litter the lake," said Rose. "My guess is it was an outsider."

"I hope you're right," said Ava. "I don't like the thought of our neighbors littering."

"Or committing murder," said Arlen.

"That, too."

"There's no proof he was on the lake. He could easily have been on the west road. Much as I dislike the thought, Mr. Zader remains on the suspect list," said Arlen. "Next is Wandalene Brackett."

"I can't see her shooting her best friend," said Rose. "When Burklie, Ana Sofia, and I picked up odds and ends from her, it looked as if she had been crying. She's definitely grieving."

"That she is," said Arlen. "It could also be remorse, so let's not let that cloud our judgment. Statistically, as Rose likes to point out, more people are killed by those closest to them than by strangers."

"What about means?" asked Rose.

Olivia looked up from her laptop. "She has several guns registered to her, including a .22 pistol. She's a member of an exclusive gun club near the city. Shoots skeet, mostly for charity events, but sometimes in local competitions."

"That's interesting," said Arlen. "So, means is a yes. Motive is anger, as evidenced by the fierce argument they had on Sunday. She was adamant that Mrs. May divorce her husband."

"Can't fault her for that," said Rose.

"Not for having an opinion," said Ava. "But it's not seemly to comment on another person's marriage to their face. Even if they are old friends, that crossed a line in my mind."

"She was just warning her," argued Rose. "I wish my friends had warned me about my ex. Maybe then I wouldn't have to---"

Her face turned red, and she looked down at her hands.

"Have to what?" asked Arlen. Ava shot him a glare and Truly shook his head slightly.

"Never mind," said Arlen. "We're getting off track. What about opportunity? The phone call to Mrs. May came from her home landline."

"We only have her word for it that she slept until eight o'clock and someone broke in and made the call," said Truly. "She could have lied about that and called her friend to meet her in an out-of-the-way place on the west side. She shot her, then showed up at the May's house while you were there and put on a show of being shocked."

"That's possible," said Arlen.

He took a step back and stared at the whiteboard. "In theory, any one of them could have done it. Or none of them."

Truly made a fresh column on the board and placed a question mark at the top. "This is for person or persons unknown. We really need more solid evidence."

"That we do," said Arlen. "Olivia, any word from Dr. Concord?"

"Just this minute got her email," said Olivia as she clacked at her keyboard. "Forwarding the autopsy report to all of you."

Arlen checked his laptop and scrolled through the report. "She managed to narrow the time frame. No question that Mrs. May was dead before eight o'clock Tuesday morning. Murder weapon was a .22 pistol, like we thought. Body was rolled down into the ditch. Not a scrap of new information that we can use."

"The time confirms that our three prime suspects all had the opportunity to shoot Mrs. May," said Truly.

Arlen closed his eyes and rubbed his temples. "I wonder who else was out and about at that time of day? Ava, I hate to say it, but I think we need to send the village a text request for information. Ask them if they saw anyone near the west side of the lake on Tuesday morning between six and nine."

"I'll do it now," Ava said. "I'll log the responses on our system. We might also catch some people at the village's memorial service for Mrs. May."

"What time is that?" asked Arlen.

"Tomorrow morning, nine o'clock. Giddy Hutton insisted that we get it over with early so the village can focus on the final details for next week's festival."

Arlen winced. "That's a might callous."

"It is, and I blistered her ears for it," Ava huffed. "Those two never got along, probably because Mrs. May refused to let Giddy push her around. Still, that's no excuse to disrespect the dead. I'm not standing for that."

"None of us should. I can't imagine Miss Giddy took kindly to being scolded."

Ava tilted her head. "Come to think of it, she took it extremely well. In fact, she's been buttering me up all week. Heaven only knows what she's got in store for me. Guess we'll find out at Saturday's festival meeting."

"Another one?"

"Yes, sir. Eleven a.m. sharp. Mandatory attendance."

Arlen groaned. "It's not like we have a murder to solve or anything."

There was a light rap on the door and Gavyn poked his head in. "Chief Well, Miss Burklie and Ana Sofia are out front and would like a word. They look shaken up."

Arlen rushed to the front room and found Burklie sitting in a chair with Ana Sofia standing over her holding her hand. He knelt in front of Burklie who was indeed shaking.

"What's wrong, Burklie? What's happened? Are you alright?"

She winced and nodded her head. Ana Sofia answered for her. "We were caught off guard, that's all, Chief Well."

Truly jumped in. "Did someone hurt you? Tell me where they went."

Ava pushed Arlen and Truly aside. "For goodness' sake, give these ladies some air. Go on, Ana Sofia. Tell us what happened."

"Burklie and I were at the village hall sorting through the odds and ends that Rose helped us gather. Thank you for that, Rose."

Rose beamed at her. "My pleasure."

"Get on with it, Sugar," said Ava.

"We were folding the clothes and weeding out the ones that looked raggedy. We came across this pretty silk kerchief, pale yellow with little red roses on it. Miss Burklie held it up and said the roses on one side didn't look right."

"I didn't have my glasses on," said Burklie. "I passed it to Ana Sofia to let her young eyes take a gander."

Ana Sofia nodded. "I looked closely and almost fainted on the spot. Looked to me like drops of blood."

"Where is the kerchief now?" asked Arlen.

"I left it in the box on the far-left table in the hall, and we came here quick as we could. It might be nothing, but I confess this murder has spooked us a little."

"You did the right thing," said Arlen. "Truly and Rose, you're with me. Ava---"

"Take care of the ladies, I know. I've got some chamomile tea that will settle their nerves right down. Y'all come with me."

"Gavyn, take their statements, please, after they finish their tea, in case this turns out to be related to Mrs. May."

"Yes, sir."

As they entered the village hall, Arlen saw half a dozen villagers swarming around getting things set up for next week's festival.

"Truly---"

"Get everyone's name and have them leave the hall until we're done here."

"I don't know why I bother talking when y'all got it all figured out."

Truly laughed and headed off to handle the festival volunteers.

"Rose, that looks like the box over to the left. Is that one that you folks picked up?"

"I can't be sure, Chief. Might ring a bell if I looked at the other items in the box."

"You have gloves?"

Rose pulled latex gloves out of her coat pocket. "Always."

"Good. Let's see what we've got."

Before they could take two steps, Giddy Hutton came charging up. "Hold on there, Arlen Well! What do you mean by busting in here and ordering us out? Need I remind you the festival is in one week?"

"Can't be helped, Miss Giddy," said Arlen. "Official police business. Now if you would kindly step outside, we'd be much obliged."

"I don't have time for this!"

Arlen wanted to throw that statement back at her, but he was mindful of his manners. "I'd appreciate it, Miss Giddy, if you'd find it in your heart to make time. Unless there's some reason you don't want us to find Mrs. May's killer."

Giddy paled. "Why---why no, that's not what I mean at all.

But our festival has nothing to do with that! And neither do I."

Arlen noticed that Giddy was clutching the front of her sweater. "I'm not saying you did. No doubt you were tucked up in your house while all that mischief was going on."

"That's exactly where I was! Home all morning."

"Excuse me, Miss Giddy," said Rose. "That's not true. I got to your place at six o'clock to work in the greenhouse and you left shortly after that. I think you've gotten the days mixed up. Meaning no disrespect, ma'am."

Giddy swayed a little. Arlen instinctively took a step forward to catch her if she fainted, but she recovered herself.

She cleared her throat. "Mixed up? Why, Rose, honey, I think you're right. I'm such a goose! That was the day I went to the city for---I mean, on festival business."

"You do so much for the village, Miss Giddy," said Arlen. "Understandable that you'd mix up the days."

"That's kind of you to say."

"Why don't you go over to the station and ask Ava for a cup of tea? I promise we'll be out of here before you know it."

Giddy pursed her lips. "Seeing as how I don't have much of a choice, I'll accept your kind invitation."

She turned on her heels and flounced out. Rose shrugged. "That one runs hot and cold."

"I can't disagree with you there. Let's get to that box, shall we? Ana Sofia said it was on the far left, correct?"

"That's what she said, but I don't see a kerchief on that box. Wait! There it is, on the box behind it and to the right."

"Take pictures of it and the surrounding area, Rose, before we touch anything. I see Truly is done talking to the volunteers, so I'll have him take pictures of the rest of the hall."

"You got it."

After the photographs were taken, the three of them approached the box. Something seemed off to Arlen. "Do y'all notice anything strange about this kerchief?"

Truly stared at it, then shook his head. Rose frowned, then opened her eyes wide and snapped her fingers. "It's folded! Didn't Ana Sofia say she dropped it and rushed over to the station? If she was freaked out because of the murder, I don't think she'd stop to fold it up."

"I think the kerchief's been moved," said Arlen. "The ladies said it was in the far-left box. We found it in the middle of the row and to the back."

"Yeah," said Truly. "Ana Sofia's too smart to make that big of a mistake."

"I think we can agree that someone folded the kerchief and put it in a different box than the one it was originally found in. Correct?"

"Agreed," said Truly.

"It's obvious," said Rose. "The question is was it on purpose or an innocent mistake?"

"We don't know yet," said Arlen. "Truly, go back to each volunteer and ask them. Get a statement from everyone as to who they remember being in the village hall for the past hour or so."

"On it."

"Rose, let's take a closer look at the kerchief. Do you have your UV light?"

Rose nodded, then carefully unfolded the scarf and ran the light over it. It revealed a splatter of dried drops of blood. She looked at Arlen and then placed it in an evidence bag.

"Take it to the city and ask their forensics team to analyze it as quickly as they can."

"On my way."

"Wait, Rose. First, look at these boxes---this one and the one to the far left---and tell me if you remember picking up any of these items when you went out with Burklie and Ana Sofia."

Rose rummaged carefully through the box on the far left. "This is full of mish-mash we picked up from the east cottages and a few of the homes just outside the village center. I don't know who gave what exactly. I've never seen this scarf before. It's a pretty color and I would have remembered. Sorry."

"That's okay. Did Mr. Zader give any donations?"

Rose snorted. "A jar of rusty fishhooks. He said manning the table year after year was donation enough."

"I see. What about this other box?"

Rose lifted the carefully folded winter clothes, then nodded her head. "Yes, I remember this one. High quality clothes, barely worn. I made a mental note to buy this cashmere sweater first thing when the festival opens. Can't believe anyone would throw this away."

"Who gave these clothes?"

Rose stared at Arlen for a second. "Ms. Brackett. You don't think---?"

"We don't know what to think at this point. We need facts. Get it to the lab in the city and we'll go from there."

As Rose turned to leave, Daxton May entered the hall and practically ran up to them.

"It's all over the village that you've found new evidence, Chief Well. Is that it?"

Arlen held up his hand. "First, tell me where you heard this."

"Nova and some of the ladies outside were concerned---they're such sweethearts---and suggested I ask you. So, have you found Niralya's killer, or are you on one of your famous breaks?"

He laughed and hit his hand on his thigh. "Kidding!"

Rose waved her hands around. "Do you see a killer in here? Do you need a mirror?"

"Rose, that will do," said Arlen.

Rose glared. Mr. May scoffed, "You know, you'd look prettier if you'd smile."

"And you'd look smarter if you were quiet."

"Excuse me?"

"Yeah, it's like every time you open your mouth the dum-

dums fall out. Ever seen a broken gumball machine? Chiclets falling all over the floor. It's like that."

"You don't have to insult me."

"Agree to be disagreeable."

Mr. May turned to Arlen. "Are you going to let this female talk to me like that?"

Arlen lifted his eyebrows. "I'm sorry. Must have been on my break."

Mr. May started to sputter and Arlen once again raised his hand. "Get out, Mr. May. If I need to interview you again, I'll let you know."

Mr. May stalked out of the hall. Arlen put his hands on his hips and turned to Rose. "Dum-dums, Rose?"

"Hey, if the gumball fits!"

Arlen shook his head. "Get on to the city, will you? Call Gavyn on your way and ask him to come over with an extra blue light."

"Yes, sir."

Arlen, Truly, and Gavyn ran the light over every item in the boxes on the left side of the hall but didn't find any other signs of blood. Arlen's back started to ache, and his stomach rumbled.

"We should take a break," he said.

"The other items in the hall are large enough that Gavyn and I can finish this on our own. Why don't you get something to eat and we'll meet you back at the station in a little bit?"

"Thank you. I expect Ava's got something prepared for you two as well. By the way, Gavyn, I forgot to ask if you and Mr. Zader found anything in the lake?"

Gavyn's eyes got big. "Yes, sir! I clean forgot when I saw Miss Burklie that upset and then all this searching for blood. I put it in the incident room, bagged and tagged, like how Cashel taught me."

"Put what, son?"

"The gun. A .22 pistol."

9

EARLY THE NEXT MORNING ARLEN AND TRULY MET IN THE incident room to brainstorm as they chowed down on the breakfast that Arlen brought in foil-covered paper plates. Ava took one look at the burnt toast and greasy fried eggs and raised her eyebrows. Without a word, she snatched their plates and replaced them with steaming bowls of shrimp and grits, fresh fruit salad, and buttermilk biscuits.

"Can any of my cooking be salvaged, Ava?"

"Nope. But the dogs thank you."

She stormed out of the room and Arlen sighed. "I ought to have known better."

Truly laughed. "I would have eaten it, but my standards are not as high as Ava's."

"No one's are. Okay, let's get started."

"Rose and Gavyn are driving back from the city. They stayed the night at Gavyn's aunt's house. She has three empty guest rooms, and she was tickled to have the company."

"We should send her something for her trouble."

Ava carried in a large urn of coffee and Truly jumped to help her place it on the side table. "You know better than to think I'd send those young'uns to the city without provisions. I made up a

86

basket of sandwiches and baked goods, plus my canned preserves and a big ole bag of pecans for his aunt."

"Don't know why I doubted you, Ava."

"You'll learn one day, I 'spect," she muttered as she walked back to the front of the station.

As they ate, Arlen stared at the whiteboard. "We don't want to twiddle our thumbs waiting for reports from the city. What else can we do to figure this out?"

"We'll be watching folks at the village funeral---I mean Mrs. May's funeral that the villagers attend, not a funeral for the village. Sorry, Chief, my brain ain't woke up yet."

"Grab another cup of coffee. Fact is, we're not used to this pace nor the extra hours."

Arlen patted his full stomach. "We might need to focus on our fitness, too. By we, I mean me, 'cause you young people go running together of a morning, don't you?"

Truly blushed. "Not this week, to tell the truth. We'll get back to it once the case is solved."

"No telling when that will be. Do what you have to do to stay healthy and strong."

Ava breezed in to put a fresh bud vase in the center of the table. "That's the collards calling the lettuce green. Are you taking care of yourself, Arlen Well? Hmm?"

"I could ask the same thing, Ava Corbridge, seeing as how you're here before me every morning---with, I might add, enough homecooked food to feed a small army. I'm not entirely sure you're mortal."

Ava grinned broadly. "I'm giving you a pass on that back chat, 'cause it's a sweet sentiment. Now go on and catch this killer before I bill the village for a new stove! All this cooking...I swanny."

Truly chuckled after Ava left the room. "You'd best be care-ful, Chief. Not wise to trifle with the real boss of the station."

"Boss of the whole village, more like. And we're lucky to

have her. Anyway, let's get back to the case at hand. Why was Mrs. May killed? Why now? What made someone desperate enough to take her life?"

"If we ask who benefits, it's obviously the husband," said Truly. "Unhappy in his marriage; in dire straits for mind-boggling sums of money. His motives are strong."

"Agreed. He had access to guns as well."

Truly tapped his pen on the table. "Opportunity is iffy, but not impossible. He knew the household staff would be out of the house, so he didn't worry about being seen. Mrs. May's routine never varied, and she would arrive at the east cottages by eight o'clock every Tuesday. He could have used some pretense to coax her into going to the west side first, maybe saying she would have plenty of time to make it to the cottages by eight."

"Sounds plausible. What about the phone call that morning?"

"Let's see. He could have made the call from Ms. Brackett's house---you know, for misdirection. He tells his wife a story about his car breaking down on the west side and needing a ride home. He lures her there, shoots her, then drives like a demon to the city. He may have taken the antique gun earlier and had it with him, so there was no need for him to return home."

"All entirely possible. You know, I can't help but wish we had video cameras on the main road to prove what time he actually left for the city."

Truly winced. "Yeah, but spying on our neighbors is creepy."

"Murder is creepier."

"True. As for the others, I don't see how Mr. Zader or Ms. Brackett's arguments with Mrs. May would rise to such a level that they'd meticulously plan her murder."

"I agree about Mr. Zader. Mrs. May being dead wouldn't necessarily mean the eviction would stop. Her husband could pick up where she left off. Mr. Zader seemed genuinely surprised when he was allowed to stay in his house."

"Yep. I might be biased because I've known the man all my

life, but he's never been violent or conniving. I can't see him sneaking into Ms. Brackett's house and calling Mrs. May to meet him on the west road. Much less shooting her in cold blood. It's not in his character."

"Probably not in her character to meet him there, either, that time of morning." Arlen pointed to the whiteboard. "What about Ms. Brackett? Her emotions were mighty tangled up after that argument on Sunday."

"She loved Mrs. May but was thwarted and couldn't show it openly. Fear of scandal and judgment are the real evils if you ask me. Folks ought to be free to live their lives if they ain't hurting nobody."

"No argument there."

"Folks shouldn't be bullied to be this way or that way. If they're in love, great. And, if they're not ready for marriage, then so be it. Folks need to stay in their lane."

Arlen wasn't going to touch that last comment with a ten-foot pole. "Love can turn to hate fairly quickly if it's unrequited. Ms. Brackett got fed up and the argument on Sunday may have sent her over the edge."

Truly ticked off points with his fingers. "The phone call to Mrs. May came from her home landline. She has no verifiable alibi for the early morning hours. She was upset about their relationship. She demanded that Mrs. May leave her husband, which Mrs. May refused to do. The bloody kerchief was in the box of clothes she donated to the festival, assuming that's related. Plus, she matches the description of the woman who threw the gun off the pier."

"Hold up. We don't know for a fact that the woman threw the gun. Could have tossed a piece of that lake litter the Councilman is upset about. Anyone could have thrown the gun in the water at any time. Heck, we don't even know yet if this particular gun is the murder weapon. Let's not get ahead of ourselves."

Olivia walked into the room with her eyes glued to her phone.

Arlen wondered how she didn't bump into the walls or furniture. She glanced up and shot them a brief smile. "That's a lot of wild guesses and circumstantial whatnots, Chief Well, if you don't mind me saying."

"Pipe up whenever you want, Olivia. You're a valued member of this team."

"Feel free," said Truly. "We're brainstorming because we don't have any solid facts to sink our teeth into."

Olivia blushed bright red and turned her attention to her laptop. After a minute of silence, she looked up with eyes as big as saucers. "The gun they fished out of the lake was registered. To Ms. Brackett."

Truly grabbed his phone and read the email. He nodded to Arlen. "We don't have ballistics yet, but they are giving it priority. A few rounds were left in the magazine, and they have the casing we picked up for comparison. What do we do in the meantime, Chief?"

"Let's go see what Ms. Brackett has to say for herself. Under caution. Olivia, if we're not back in time for the funeral, you and the others will need to observe the crowd and take note of who's there---and who's not---and anything else that seems off."

"We'll do our best, Chief."

As Truly drove them to Ms. Brackett's house, Arlen got lost in his thoughts. He couldn't help feeling sorry for the woman. From what he understood, she had made Mrs. May the center of her life for decades, even moving to Hutton Village to be close to her. Her heart must have been broken when her dedication and affection were rebuffed. Still, murder was a step too far---if she was in fact guilty.

The house was at the dead end of a long desolate road. The property was enclosed with a high fence, though the gate was wide open. Truly parked in front effectively blocking the driveway.

"Do you notice anything in particular about this neighborhood?" Arlen asked as they approached the driveway. "Other than it's mighty quiet."

Truly looked around at the fields and gentle hills that surrounded the area. "The house is isolated. Nearest neighbor is at least a quarter mile away and trees block it from view. There's only one way in and out---no, wait!"

He ran towards an open field, then jogged back barely out of breath. "There's a dirt road across that field."

"Where does it lead?"

Truly shook his head. "Don't know for sure, but I wonder if it hooks up with the road to the west of the lake. It's headed in that direction. Want me to check it?"

"Later. Let's talk to Ms. Brackett first."

"It may be too early for her to be up and about, since she said she sleeps until eight."

Arlen walked to the front door, rang the doorbell, then stepped slightly to the right. Truly stood to the left. There was no answer other than the *wha-wha-wha* call of a wild bird.

"Is that a nuthatch?"

Truly cocked his head. "Sounds like it."

Arlen rang the doorbell again, then walked along the porch and peered into the front window. Through the frosted glass pane, he saw the drapes had been pulled back to reveal Ms. Brackett's sitting room. He blinked his eyes and looked closer. On the floor between the couch and the coffee table lay a woman.

"Truly, she's on the floor! Break the door and I'll call it in."

Truly turned the doorknob. "It's not locked, Chief."

They rushed inside as Arlen called Ava to dispatch Dr. Concord to their location. Truly felt for a pulse.

"She's alive. Breathing is shallow. Should we drive her to the clinic?"

Arlen passed that information on to Ava, then hung up. "No, Kathleen is five minutes out. She's on her way back from a house call and passing this way. Let's note our preliminary observations while we wait."

"She's wearing night clothes. There's a cup of tea on the table with a bottle of pills next to it. No label."

"We'll bag those. But first, please check the upstairs and all the other rooms. No telling what we've walked in on."

By the time Truly came back to report the house was clear, Dr. Concord had hastily examined Ms. Brackett. "She's stable but weak. We should get her to the hospital in the city as soon as possible. I've got a foldable stretcher with wheels, but I can't do transport. My van is full of puppies."

"Puppies? What in tarnation?"

"That was my house call. To pick up the Springers' beagles and bring them in to be microchipped. The family's got their hands full helping with the funeral lunch and the festival set up, so I offered to get the pups."

"Okay, well that can't be helped. Truly, we'll put Ms. Brackett in your car. Y'all take her to the hospital fast as you can. Lights and siren after you get clear of the village. Radio the highway patrol for an escort, if they can oblige. I'll watch the puppies until help arrives."

After they left, Arlen looked through the window of the van and saw five little balls of fur curled up together on a fleece blanket fast asleep. Not a care in the world.

He tiptoed away and called Ava. "I need---"

"Gavyn and Rose at the Brackett house. Already rerouted them. They'll be there within the hour."

"Thank you. We'll also need---"

"A search warrant for Ms. Brackett's property. Olivia is on the radio with Cashel getting the details and she'll send it to Judge Tanner in a few minutes."

"Very good. Will---"

"Olivia and I watch folks at the funeral? Of course. I deputized my husband, Burklie, and Ana Sofia to help us. We're covered on this end."

"Thank Nate and the ladies for me. Last thing---"

"The Springer boys are on their way to get the puppies and take Kathleen's van to her clinic. Anything else?"

"Nope. Like I always say, you're a treasure."

"You're not wrong."

"Beats me what y'all need me for."

"We need you put on your thinking cap and figure out what's going on. One woman dead, another close to it. The village isn't going to stand for much more of this."

"Any responses to our request for information?"

"Nothing useful so far. We'll ask around at the funeral."

"Don't let on what happened to Ms. Brackett."

"Land o' Goshen! Do you know who you're talking to? Only excuse I'll accept is you're distracted trying to decide which puppy to take!"

She hung up before Arlen could protest. He went back to the van and found the puppies awake and tussling with each other. One plump pup remained nestled in the warm blanket but had its eyes open watching the fray. It looked at Arlen and yawned.

"Not saying I am, but if I had to choose, it would be you."

A few hours later, Arlen gathered his team in the living room of the house. "What have we found so far?"

"Ms. Brackett's not as obsessively organized as Mrs. May," said Rose. "But her house is clean and well-maintained. We recovered the teacup and its contents, plus the bottle of pills. I bagged all the tea in the pantry and all the kitchen trash. Do you want me to run them into the city?"

"No, I'll do that," said Arlen. "I need to relieve Truly at the hospital. I may as well swing by the police lab on the way."

"I can drive you, Chief," said Gavyn. "It will be dark before you get back. Your night vision ain't great, begging your pardon. What if you hit a deer?"

"I appreciate the concern, but I'll be fine. You've had a long day and should get some rest after we're done here. What else do we have?"

"She has a large gun safe, but we'll need tools to break it open," said Gavyn. "There was a handgun in the nightstand table in her bedroom and another one in a desk drawer in the sitting room. We bagged both of those."

"I'll ask Ms. Brackett for the combination to the safe when she wakes up," said Arlen. "No reason to bust her things unless we absolutely have to. Is that it?"

Rose hesitated. "It seems funny that the front door was unlocked. She allegedly had a recent break in, yet she didn't secure the house at night? Doesn't sound right to me."

"If she intended self-harm---and I'm not concluding yet that she did---she may have left the door open to make it easier for us to get inside. Were there any prints?"

"Wiped clean except for Cashel's on the doorknob," said Gavyn. "Ms. Brackett's prints are all over the house, as you would expect. Except for the front door, the coffee table, and the kitchen counters. Those surfaces don't have a mark on them."

"Neither does her tea kettle and it still has water in it," said Rose.

"That's odd," said Arlen. "Unless someone else made the tea and didn't want to leave their prints behind."

"That rules out Mr. May," scoffed Rose. "That idiot doesn't know how to make tea!"

10

ARLEN STOOD AT THE COUNTER IN THE CITY POLICE LAB AND smiled courteously through the plexiglass barrier at the middle-aged clerk glaring at him. Her curly frosted bob swished as she vigorously shook her head. Her colleague at the next desk, a clean-cut young man in chinos, avoided making eye contact.

"Might be a year before we even look at that mess," the clerk said. "We've got our own cases, you know."

"I'm sure you'll do your best. Sounds like a busy place."

She huffed, "Ha! You don't know the half of it."

Arlen gave her a sheepish grin and waited. She pursed her lips. "Six months would be a blessing, let me tell you!"

"I admire your dedication. Your work is critical to the community."

The clerk put both hands on her hips and frowned. "A month on the outside if we hop like jackrabbits---which is a huge imposition. This is the city, not some backwater in the sticks!"

"I appreciate that, Mrs....?"

She blinked. "Miss. Miss Agnes Allmond. Two Ls."

Arlen bowed his head slightly. "Pleased to make your acquaintance, Miss Allmond."

Agnes inspected her stubby fingernails. "If we really push it, maybe two weeks. You can't expect better than that."

"Much obliged. My assistant Olivia Pepper will coordinate with you."

The young man popped his head up and squeaked, "Olivia Pepper?"

"Yes, sir. She's our village tech consultant. Do you know her?"

The young man walked to the counter. "We went to college together. She's right smart."

"She is, and I'm sure she'd say the same about you, Mr.---?"

"Caleb...Caleb Salterman."

"Pleased to know you, Mr. Salterman."

Agnes scowled and threw her hands in the air. "Guess we're all friends now! Ain't that cozy?"

Caleb grimaced slightly. "Agnes, would you like to go to dinner early? You can use a half hour of my time. I'll take this, um, problem off your hands."

"Don't have to tell me twice!" Without another word she grabbed her handbag from under her desk and headed out the door.

Caleb turned to Arlen and whispered, "Sorry about that. She's really good at her job, but doesn't have the best customer service attitude, know what I mean?"

"I'm sure Miss Allmond is utterly charming when she doesn't have hick police chiefs standing between her and her dinner."

Caleb laughed. "Yeah, no. She's...well, she's Agnes. Anyway, I'll see that the lab gets your evidence right away. There's other stuff your people brung in. We've started on some of it."

"Oh, so you met Olivia's brother Gavyn. He brought in the gun."

Caleb's smiled vanished. "That was her brother? Lawsy! Hope I didn't make a fool of myself in front of him."

"I'm sure you did fine, son. Did you speak with my other officer, Rose Tern? She brought in the kerchief."

"No, Agnes helped her. They got on like a house on fire. Laughing and carrying on. Agnes fast-tracked that scarf, too. You should have the report pretty quick."

"That's good to hear. Well, I'll be getting on. Thank you, Mr. Salterman."

"Call me Caleb."

"Caleb. I'll tell Olivia I met you."

The boy froze like a deer in headlights. "Lawsy!"

On the way to the hospital, Arlen stopped at his favorite smokehouse and picked up dinner. On the rare occasions when he came to the city, he always ordered the same thing: chopped brisket, corn pudding, butterbeans, and hush puppies. Ava would likely scoff at that combination, but Arlen was starving and wanted comfort food.

As he walked in the main entrance to the hospital, he instinctively turned left towards the oncology department. He was a frequent visitor there when his wife was receiving her treatments. He stopped short, took a deep breath, and pivoted to the right. He found Truly pacing up and down a corridor.

Arlen pointed towards the emergency department as he handed Truly the sack of food. "Is she still in there?"

Truly peeked inside the bag and inhaled deeply. "No, they moved her to a private room a few hours ago. She's awake, but they won't let me talk to her yet. I'm just…"

"Guarding the hallway?" They looked around at the empty walkway.

"Pretty much."

"Is there a place we can eat our dinner?"

"There's a waiting room with tables and chairs a little ways down."

"Good enough. Let's go."

Truly used paper napkins as placemats and set the basket of

hush puppies in the middle of the table. They ate in companionable silence for a few minutes.

"This is almost as good as Ana Sofia's brisket."

"That a fact?"

"She's a good cook. Truth is she's pretty much good at everything."

"You don't sound happy about that."

"I am. It's just…"

"What's going on, Cashel?"

Truly blinked at Arlen's rare use of his first name. "She turned me down."

"What?"

"I pre-proposed marriage and she turned me down."

"What does pre-propose mean?"

"I asked her what she'd think about me possibly proposing one day and she said no."

"No forever or no right now?"

"I'm not sure. She's acting the same, but I don't know where we go from here."

"Be patient. Ana Sofia is a sensible woman. You may have caught her off guard. Set a time to talk with her and really listen to what she has to say."

"Yeah, I 'spect you're right."

Truly stared at the wall and Arlen let him sit with his thoughts. After a few minutes, Truly cleared his throat and got back to business.

"Do we have enough to charge Ms. Brackett?"

Arlen considered. "Not even close. Like Olivia pointed out, it's all circumstantial."

"That stunt with the pills looks like an admission of guilt."

"I'd expect that from Rose, but you should know better. It could have been an accident, or…"

"Someone tried to kill her. The question is why?"

"Unclear at this point. We need to speak with her as soon as she's able. Is there a nurse in charge that we can ask?"

"The head nurse doesn't talk."

"Did you show her your badge?"

"No, I mean, she sings her sentences instead of talking like a normal person."

Arlen laughed. "Nurse Harmony's still here? She was my wife's favorite nurse. Made things pleasant, especially...towards the end. It will be good to see her again."

A lilting hum floated in from the hall and was soon followed by a nurse in dark purple scrubs bedazzled with neon green kitten decals. Around her neck she wore three strands of multi-colored light up beads shaped like butterflies. She took one look at Arlen and broke out in song.

"*Heard a man went fishin' but only caught a guppy. If'n he wants a favor, he best share a hush puppy!*"

Arlen grinned as he lifted the basket of hush puppies. She took one and popped it in her mouth.

"Good to see you again, Nurse Harmony. You light up every room you enter. Literally."

She winked at him as she chewed her food, then pulled a small water bottle out of her pocket and washed it down.

"*Them's pretty good, but I don't know why, I liked to choke 'cause this batch is dry.*"

"Sorry about that. I expect they got cold."

Arlen pointed at Truly. "You've met my sergeant. We're here---"

She snatched a paper off her clipboard and waved it in the air. "*I heard tell all about your capers, but to talk to my lady, y'all gone need these papers.*"

She handed the papers to Truly and grabbed another hush puppy. The sound of melodic humming faded as she walked down the corridor.

Truly stared at the door with his mouth open. "She's…something."

"That she is. Let's see what she brought us."

"It's a consent for you and me to visit with Ms. Brackett. Oh, wow. She also gives the hospital permission to show us her medical records. That's surprising."

"Could be a couple of things. One, she trusts us. Two, she's innocent and is doing everything in her power to prove it. Not that she's obligated to."

"Or, three, she's covered her tracks so well that she thinks we're not going to find proof of her crime."

"You're getting cynical in your old age, Sergeant," Arlen chuckled. "I approve. That trait might save you one day from making a fool of yourself."

"I need all the help I can get," Truly muttered and gathered up their dinner things.

Nurse Harmony was tapping at the computer at the nurses' station and beckoned Arlen over. She didn't say---or sing---anything, though she was humming what sounded like a spiritual. It was comforting. She pointed to the screen and Arlen read the information.

They walked quietly into Ms. Brackett's room. Arlen placed a chair next to the bed and Truly sat on a folding chair in a corner.

Ms. Brackett looked pale and weak. She held out her hand. Arlen took it in both of his and gave it a gentle shake. She smiled faintly. "You saved my life again, Chief Well. Thank you."

"You're welcome. Do you feel up to talking or would you prefer to wait?"

"Let's talk now, though I warn you I'm still fuzzy."

"Take your time. If you need rest, we'll leave and come back tomorrow."

She shook her head. "I want to know what happened."

"That's our question to you."

She coughed softly and adjusted her blanket. "I'm not sure.

Last thing I remember is making a cup of tea late Friday evening. Then, I woke up here and everyone is tiptoeing around giving me fake smiles and acting as if I'm loony."

"Do you remember how many pills you took?"

"Pills? I didn't take any pills! You took away my bottle at the lake, remember?"

Arlen patted her hand. "People always say 'stay calm' which I generally find patronizing, but it might fit in this case. How about I tell you what we found and see if we can piece together what happened. Okay?"

She nodded and brushed away a tear.

"Sergeant Truly and I came to your house to talk to you early this morning. You didn't answer the door, so I peeked in your front window and saw you on the floor. The door was unlocked--"

"Unlocked? No! I locked that door before I got ready for bed."

"Does anyone else have a key to your house?"

The tears spilled out of her eyes, but she made no move to wipe them. "Only Niralya. I'm not imagining things, Chief Well. I locked that door!"

Arlen reached for a box of tissue on the side table and handed it to her. "I understand. Let me continue, please."

She nodded as she dried her face. "I'm sorry."

"We entered through the unlocked front door, found that you were alive, thank heavens, and called Dr. Concord to check you. She and Sergeant Truly brought you to the hospital. We saw the teacup on the coffee table and a bottle of pills next to it."

"They're not mine."

"We got a search warrant and confiscated---temporarily, mind you---your two handguns."

"Three. I have three handguns. One in my bedroom and two in the desk in my sitting room."

Truly looked up from his notes, but Arlen raised his hand to stop him from speaking. "When did you last see your handguns?"

"The one in the nightstand in my bedroom I checked after my bath and before I went downstairs to make the tea. My house settles sometimes, and I heard a noise."

"What type of noise?"

"Hard to describe. Like a scraping. Metallic sounding. I chalked it up to nerves and went on to make the tea."

"Did you check your doors after that?"

Ms. Brackett looked sheepish. "Only the back door. I knew I had locked the front door earlier when my company left."

"What company?"

"First, that Hutton woman and a couple of her cronies showed up around four o'clock. I didn't want to be rude, so I let them come in for a while."

"Please tell me Miss Giddy wasn't hounding you about the festival."

"Surprisingly, no. It was strange. She expressed concern for the loss of my friend, then offered to have Miss Green and the other lady---a Mrs. Springer, I think---take over all of my festival duties."

"That was considerate."

"They were beyond polite, though it seemed forced---except for Mrs. Springer. She seemed genuinely concerned. That Miss Green was quite uppity, though, and it looked to me like Mrs. Hutton had to bite her tongue a few times. Might have just been my imagination, but they seemed annoyed with each other."

"Probably what we call 'festival nerves.' Tell me, did they go into any other part of your house?"

Ms. Brackett considered. "Each of them at some point used the powder room next to the kitchen and Mrs. Hutton helped me bring in the tea things. I told her I could manage, but she insisted."

"Were any of them left alone in the sitting room?"

"Possibly. I didn't have my eye on them the whole time. Besides going to the kitchen, I went upstairs to retrieve my festival notes and things. Mrs. Springer helped me carry a box of decorations down the stairs."

"Had any of them been to your house before?"

"All of them in the last couple of months regarding festival plans. I didn't socialize with them other than that. Niralya was always there for the meetings, too."

"Did Lincoln Zader ever visit?"

Ms. Brackett smiled. "Yes, a couple of times to take some odds and ends off my hands. He's a character. I like him."

"He is that. Going back to the handguns, when was the last time you saw the two you kept in your sitting room?"

Ms. Brackett looked up at the ceiling. "Ages ago. I can't remember because I haven't had any reason to use them. I use my shotgun when I shoot skeet."

"May we have the combination to your gun safe?"

Truly handed her a piece of notepaper and she wrote the numbers on it.

"Thank you, Ms. Brackett," Truly said. "If you don't mind my asking, did anyone else visit you on Friday? You said 'first', and I wondered what was second."

"Yes, that man had the nerve to drop in. Uninvited."

"Which man," asked Arlen.

"Dax. I'm sorry, but I really cannot stand him."

"Did he upset you?"

"He tried to be charming, but I saw that for the manipulation it was. Then, he brought up the will."

"Were you mentioned in her will?"

"Yes, she left me a nice sum. I didn't know about that until her lawyer called me after her death."

"What did Mr. May have to say about the will?"

"How he'd been told that if I renounce the share that Niralya left me, it will go to him. He thought that was fair since he was the widower, and I was just a friend. Ha! Just a friend."

"What did you tell him?"

"He pulled out some paper and expected me to sign it then and there! I wasn't rude, but I refuse to argue with fools. I told him firmly that I would discuss it with my attorney. That didn't go over well."

"I imagine not."

"I wouldn't budge and there was nothing more to say, so he went away. I watched through the window as he got in the car, and they left. Then, I'm sure I locked the front door. I'd swear to it."

"They? Was someone with him?"

"Yes, but I don't know who. He got in the passenger side. I didn't see the driver. It was too dark."

"Last question for tonight. What are your plans after they discharge you?"

Ms. Brackett cocked her head to one side. "You know, I'm not sure. I know I need therapy given all that's happened. There's a residential program on a private estate near the city that I'm considering. It's expensive, but I think it would be a good use of Niralya's money. She left me a lot more than I expected, but I've decided now I'm keeping it. Does that sound callous?"

"No, it sounds appropriate."

Truly piped up, "How's the security there?"

Ms. Brackett looked stricken. "Why do you ask that? I'm telling you I did not intentionally try to harm myself. Chief, please believe me!"

"I do believe you, Ms. Brackett. The problem is that someone broke into your house---again---and put sedatives in your tea."

"I might have just fallen and can't remember!"

"No, ma'am. I saw the toxicology report right before we came in. You had sedatives in your system. We're still waiting for all the forensic reports, but for now, your safety is our top concern."

"Even if the facility has security," said Truly. "You might consider hiring a private guard temporarily until we sort all this out."

Ms. Brackett crossed her arms. "I'm not comfortable having a stranger follow me around."

"It might be wise. Just for a short while."

"If anything, I'll allow that sweet, demure girl to stay with me. That's if you can spare her."

Arlen frowned. "Not sure who you mean. Sweet, demure?"

"Why that lovely girl. Rose!"

11

TRULY SLIPPED INTO THE PEW AND NODDED TO ARLEN JUST AS THE congregation finished the first hymn. Arlen listened sporadically to the pastor's message, but his mind wandered to the facts of the case. The killer had muddied the waters and wasted their time. But perhaps the solution was simpler than they thought. A theory began to take shape in his head, though he wasn't sure how to prove it. He tapped his fingers on his hymn book. He needed the forensic reports.

After the service, the villagers gathered in the church hall for snacks and hot drinks before heading home. Arlen grabbed a cup of coffee and stood alone, watching the folks around him. Across the room, he noticed Truly standing with Ana Sofia. He appeared to be listening to her, but Arlen could see his eyes also scanning the crowd. *Good man.*

Ava walked up and handed Arlen a cheese biscuit.

"Paper napkin, Ava? Are you feeling okay?"

"I don't have time for jokes, Arlen Well. I have a gaggle of boys to teach how to bake, so take your biscuit and be grateful."

"I am. Are you leaving now?"

"Yes. I need to put some distance between myself and certain people before I say something I oughtn't on a Sunday!"

"Who's drawn your fire today?"

"I've said it before, and I'll say it again. Fawning over a recent widower is unseemly. Call me judgmental, but that's how I feel."

"I expect you're right. Looks like Nate is waving at you from the door."

"He's got the car warmed up. See you later this afternoon, four o'clock. Mandatory festival meeting for the leaders."

"I'm not a festival leader."

"You are now. Y'all be on time. And mind you eat something more than that biscuit. Grown man can't even feed himself properly. I swanny."

Arlen watched her weave through the crowd, then as she suggested, turned his thoughts to lunch. He wondered if she would approve of the canned stew that he planned to heat up. Probably not. As he turned to leave, Dax May sauntered up.

Arlen nodded. "Mr. May."

"I see you're working hard on the case, Chief Well, biscuit in hand."

Arlen detected a slight smirk. "People don't live on air, Mr. May."

Dax waved his hand dismissively. "Obviously, and I don't blame you. I love a good meal. The buffet the ladies put on after Niralya's service yesterday was outstanding. You should have been there. Come to think of it, why weren't you there?"

"I was elsewhere."

"What does that mean?"

"I was someplace else which is why I couldn't be there. You of all people should understand being in a different place than the location in question."

Dax blinked. "I can never tell if you're intentionally provoking me."

Arlen simply smiled, then bit into his biscuit. He turned away as a group of young women came up and surrounded Dax, clamoring for his attention.

After a minute or two of what sounded to Arlen like nonsensical conversation and giggling, Nova Green came up and put her hand on Dax's arm. "Dax, honey, why don't you and the girls come to my house for lunch? I made apple stack cake for dessert."

That earned her a lot of oohs and aahs, and the group headed out the door without giving Arlen a second glance. Joe Solina walked over shaking his head.

"I don't remember getting that kind of attention after I lost my wife. Not that I would have welcomed it. Did you?"

Arlen shook his head. "No. And, not to gossip, but Ava says it's unseemly. Gotta agree with her there. Still, none of my business."

"I would argue that anything to do with that man is your business until you find out what happened to Mrs. May."

"You may be right."

"By the way, you're coming to our house for lunch."

"No, I don't want to put you out. I'll grab something before getting back to work."

"We insist. Cashel will be there as well as Burklie. We know y'all can't stay long, but at least you'll have a decent meal to carry you through the afternoon."

"In that case, I accept. I figure Ava put you up to it. What did she cook?"

"She sent over chicken pastry and garden peas, but I made the salad and cornbread. Ana Sofia made apple fritters for dessert to go with Burklie's home-churned pecan ice cream."

The pecan ice cream clinched it. "Still, I can't show up with empty hands. I'll run home and see what I can put together."

"No time for that. You and Cashel can wash up the dishes before you go to work. That's a fair exchange."

Arlen did his best to enjoy the meal with his friends, despite the case being on his mind. He was careful to limit his portion sizes as there was no doubt that he'd put on a few pounds recently. He blamed Ava and the villagers who had supplied them with covered dishes all week, but he knew no one forced him to take second helpings.

"More ice cream, Arlen?" asked Burklie.

Arlen sighed. "I should say no, but it's so good. Just a small scoop or I won't fit through the door."

Ana Sofia added an apple fritter to his dish. "It's the last one and you get the honors."

"Thank you kindly. I am spoiled rotten around here, let me tell you."

"You and Cashel need your strength. There's a pile of dishes in the kitchen just waiting for you."

Truly stood up from the table. "I'll get a start on them while you finish your dessert."

"I'll help you," said Joe. "Grab an apron."

"That wasn't our deal," Arlen protested. "Let us wash them."

"You sit and enjoy the company of these young ladies," Joe winked. "They'll be more inclined to gossip if we're not in the room."

"We don't gossip, Papa!" Ana Sofia pouted her lips, but her eyes were smiling.

"Impart village goings on, then. If that makes you feel better."

Burklie topped off their coffees and Arlen noticed a slight frown. "Something wrong, Burklie?"

She glanced at Ana Sofia who nodded. "Despite Joe's teasing, we don't like to gossip. Still, there's a few things we noticed when we were collecting the odds and ends. Not sure if it's important or not."

"Why don't you tell me, and we'll see what we can make of it?"

"Well, what stands out to me the most is how Giddy Hutton is not herself this week."

"Festival nerves?"

Ana Sofia shook her head. "It's more of a power imbalance. She's her usual assertive self until Nova Green comes around, then she defers to anything Nova says. No matter how ridiculous."

"Yes," added Burklie. "Then Nova will smirk like she's got something on Giddy. It's got rise-of-a-new-queen-bee vibes."

"Ashamed to say that I'm enjoying having Miss Giddy come down a notch," said Ana Sofia. "But not at the price of Nova rising."

Arlen took a small notebook from his pocket and jotted down notes as Burklie continued. "Agreed. Like it or not, there's a social hierarchy in the village and people will not take kindly to a relative newcomer taking over. For all their quirks, the Huttons do have the best interests of the village at heart."

Ana Sofia grimaced. "Then, as for Nova, there's the whole throwing herself at Mr. May that is inappropriate at best."

"Brazen is what it is. One of the older women spoke to Nova privately about it when we were sorting the odds and ends in the village hall. Nova flounced over to Giddy and announced for the whole room to hear 'I can see Dax if I want unless Miss Giddy tells me to stop!' Then Giddy said 'Why, that's your business, Nova honey.' We were floored!"

"Yeah, I mean she gave me a talking to at Christmas when the skirt I wore to church was an inch above my knee. Practically called me a hussy!" exclaimed Ana Sofia.

Arlen frowned. "Surely not."

"Ask Cashel. He was standing right beside me and snickered. Thought she was joking. The look she shot him wiped the smile off his face!"

"Sounds like this murder on top of the festival has thrown some folks off kilter," said Arlen. "Don't know what's to be done about it, but I appreciate you sharing. I expect things will get back to normal when we make an arrest."

Truly came into the dining room and held up his phone. "Hopefully that will be soon. Got a text from Rose. She, Gavyn, and Olivia are at the station. Some of the forensic reports are in. Sorry, ladies, but we need to go."

Ana Sofia gave him a peck on the cheek. "We understand, and we'll finish the dishes. But I suggest you leave the apron."

Truly blushed as he took off the frilly white cotton apron and handed it to her. Arlen headed out the door barely able to hide his grin.

The team gathered in the incident room after helping themselves to the hot coffee that Gavyn had brewed. Arlen took a sip and lifted his cup in salute to the young officer. "This is good, Gavyn. We'll be bouncing off the walls with all the caffeine, though."

The young man blushed. "It's decaf on Ava's orders. She said you can have regular iced tea with supper if you need to work late."

"Nice of her to allow me that. Okay, let's get started. Who wants to report first?"

Olivia timidly raised her hand. Arlen pointed at her. "Thank you, Olivia. What can you tell us?"

"The city lab put a rush on processing some of our evidence. They emailed preliminary results and will send us formal reports soon."

"I expect we can thank your and Rose's friends, Agnes and Caleb, for that."

Olivia blushed. "First is ballistics. Gavyn, do you want to explain it?"

"Sure. The test indicates that the gun we fished out of the lake is our weapon. No doubt about it, Chief Well."

"The gun is registered to Ms. Brackett," said Rose. "Have we eliminated her as a suspect? I'm not sure how I feel about being her bodyguard if we haven't."

"That's a fair concern," said Arlen. "Let's see what our other evidence tells us. Olivia, what's next?"

"The kerchief. It's Mrs. May's blood but they also found a few stray hairs from the person who may have worn it. Cashel, can you show the Chief the video model they sent?"

"It's an interesting model of what may have happened," said Truly. "The shooter wore the kerchief over her hair and turned her head to the left as she pulled the trigger. She must have been standing close to Mrs. May because the blood splattered back onto one side of the kerchief.

Arlen leaned over to view Truly's laptop screen. One day he'd learn to work this technology, but for today he would let his team take charge. "That's interesting. And the stray hairs? Do they know who they belong to?"

"Yes," said Olivia. "Ms. Brackett. Now that I think about it, I saw her wear that scarf to church last year. I complimented her on it. It's real pretty."

Arlen tapped his pen on the table. "So, Ms. Brackett's kerchief has Mrs. May's blood on it and Ms. Brackett's gun was used to shoot Mrs. May. The early morning phone call to Mrs. May was made from Ms. Brackett's house. They had argued a couple of days prior because Mrs. May wouldn't leave her husband. It's not looking good for Ms. Brackett, I admit."

Olivia surprised Arlen by grinning as she raised her hand again. He nodded to her. "Yes, but there's one more thing they found on it. A different stray hair."

"Oh? Do they know who that belongs to?"

"No, because it's an acrylic fiber from a wig!"

"A wig? Does Ms. Brackett wear a wig, Rose?"

"Not to my knowledge, but I'd better text Ava and see if she knows anything."

"Good, while we're waiting for---"

"She texted back. No, Ms. Brackett has never worn a wig, and none of the villagers are currently sporting wigs and haven't in recent memory."

"I tell you, y'all are way ahead of me with your texting and such."

"You know what I think?" asked Rose.

"That I'm a dinosaur?"

Rose giggled. "No. I think if the shooter wore a wig, it could have been either a man or a woman."

"True."

"That puts my favorite suspect back in the race!"

"It's not a derby, Rose."

"All I'm saying is Daxton May could have dressed up as Ms. Brackett, shot his wife, and disposed of the gun before hightailing it to the city. He presumably had access to her house and could have taken the kerchief and the gun. Might have used Mrs. May's key that Ms. Brackett gave her."

Truly jumped up and wrote on the whiteboard. "Then, he could have planted the bloodstained kerchief in the box of clothes Ms. Brackett donated to the festival. He was there that day with his flock of lady friends, and the boxes were labeled with the names of the donors."

Arlen considered. "His motive for framing her would be to disqualify her from getting anything from Mrs. May's estate. Her share would then go to him."

"Do you think that's why he tried to get her to waive her rights to the inheritance?" asked Gavyn. "Then when she wouldn't agree, he put something in her tea?"

"Oh! That reminds me," said Olivia. "There's a report on the items you recovered from Ms. Brackett's house."

"Let's hear it, please."

"A teabag in her trash contained sedatives. Enough to kill her if she had steeped the tea longer."

"How did they manage that?"

Truly scanned the emailed report. "Says here the teabag was opened, then closed back up after the sedative was inserted."

Rose tapped at her phone, then looked up. "Ava says Ms.

Brackett likes her tea weak. She steeps it for less than a minute."

"That's probably what saved her life," said Arlen. "Not enough of the sedative made it into the cup."

"Okay, but I'm going to play devil's advocate," said Truly. "What if she did that intentionally? What if she's pulling a reverse frame? Making it look like Mr. May is framing her but really, she's framing him. I wonder if she inherits his share if he is convicted of the murder."

"That's a wild theory," said Arlen. "Something Rose would dream up."

"Hey!"

"No offense, Rose, but you do have a vivid imagination." Arlen held up his hand to ward off her protests. "Creative thinking is valuable in many situations, so I am in no way disparaging you."

"Well, then…thank you."

"The problem is, although we know more than we did this morning, we still don't have enough proof to make an arrest. We'll need to interview Mr. May again. Truly and Gavyn, please bring him in. I expect you'll find him at Miss Green's house."

All the phones in the room buzzed. Truly picked up first. "No, he'll likely be at the festival meeting. Ava says it starts in fifteen minutes."

"That's even better. We can speak to some other people while we're there and clear up a few more points. We need---. Rose, are you okay?"

Rose had her hand raised but was staring at her laptop.

"Rose?"

She ignored him and gestured to Olivia to come look at her screen. Olivia squinted, then gasped. "Gavyn, look. Do you see what we see?"

Gavyn walked around the table and studied the screen. "I don't get it." Olivia pointed and Gavyn gulped. "Golly!"

The three of them turned wide eyes to Arlen and Truly.

12

As Arlen and his team walked into the festival meeting, he felt a pang of pride at how his young officers casually fanned out and took positions by the exits. Hutton Village may be a backwater in the sticks, as Agnes Allmond put it, but its peace officers could hold their own with any in the country. Arlen was more determined than ever to push for full accreditation for their little department. He envisioned the day when he could retire, turn the keys over to Truly, and go fishing.

Councilman Direberry interrupted his daydream. "Please tell me that your people are not on overtime on a Sunday! The village can't afford that, Arlen."

"The village can't afford to have a killer running loose, Chesley."

Direberry pursed his lips. "Well, I wish you'd wrap this up. Like as not it was an accident."

"Who told you that?"

"My sister mentioned that Mrs. May probably accidentally shot herself."

Arlen wanted to tell Direberry that it was highly unlikely that Mrs. May shot herself in the back of the head, then drove to the lake to toss the gun, then went back to the west side road and rolled herself into the ditch. Instead, he merely stared at the councilman until Direberry slunk away.

Giddy Hutton stepped on the raised platform and put her notes on the wooden podium. She glanced around as the villagers in attendance began to take their seats. She cleared her throat and the crowd quieted down. "Is everyone here?"

"I don't see Ms. Brackett," said Lincoln Zader. "I saved her a seat. Should we wait for her?"

Giddy frowned as Nova Green spoke up from the front row. "No, she won't be coming. She's not up to helping with the festival. Mental crisis or some such."

Arlen thought Giddy was going to bust a vein, but she took a deep breath. "It's not our place to speculate, Nova honey. If she's not well, that's all that needs to be said."

"True, Giddy *honey*, but we'd be fools not to notice how strange she's been acting all week. Why Friday when we saw her, she was positively prostrate with grief and quite despondent. No one's seen her since, and I don't mind telling you I'm worried sick."

Arlen noticed a puzzled look on Mrs. Springer's face. Rose must have seen it, too, because she walked over and sat in the chair next to her and whispered in her ear. Mrs. Springer shook her head, then frowned at Giddy and Nova. Rose returned to her place by the door and shot Arlen a look.

Arlen decided to interject. "Mr. May, how did she look to you when you visited her on Friday evening?"

Mr. May was focused on his phone but popped his head up when he heard his name. "Huh? What? I don't know what you mean."

"You were seen leaving her home Friday evening. I'm asking how she seemed at that time."

"Seen?" asked Nova. "By whom?"

Arlen ignored her and kept his gaze on Mr. May who stared openmouthed.

"Ah, Friday. Today's what? Sunday? Getting my days mixed up. Yes, well, we talked of this and that, nothing important. I left and she was perfectly fine."

"Except she was sad, right?" prompted Nova. "Grief stricken?"

Mr. May shook his head. "Maybe?"

"May I start the meeting now, please?" asked Giddy between clenched teeth.

Nova stood up. "Of course, Miss Giddy, but I ought to check on Wandalene first."

She whipped out her phone and placed the call. The hall was quiet except for Giddy tapping her pen on the podium. Nova turned to Arlen with wide eyes. "She's not answering! Someone should go to her house."

Giddy threw her hands up in the air and looked like she was going to pitch a fit, but Arlen jumped in first. "That's not necessary, Miss Green. She's not there."

Nova put her hand to her throat, but having no pearls to clutch, she fiddled with the collar of her blouse. "What do you mean, Chief Well?"

Arlen hung his head. "Sadly, she's…she's gone."

Gasps rippled throughout the village hall and chatter began until Giddy pounded on the podium to restore order. "Arlen Well, what are you talking about? Gone where?"

"Oh, Miss Giddy, isn't it obvious?" cried Nova. "She's done away with herself, probably out of guilt."

"Guilt?" asked Mr. May. "I thought you said grief?"

"Guilt, grief, what difference does it make?" Nova snapped.

Giddy paled and began to sway on the platform. Arlen dashed up to help her, but Truly beat him to it. "Someone please fetch Miss Giddy a chair and a glass of water!"

Both were provided and Giddy weakly waved her thanks. "Oh, Arlen, this is all my fault."

"How so, Miss Giddy?"

"First Niralya and now Wandalene. I'm so sorry, really I am."

"Sorry for what, ma'am?"

Mayor Hutton rushed to the platform and fussed over his wife, but she pushed him away. "Oh, Riggs, I've made a terrible mistake. Please say you'll forgive me."

The mayor hugged her. "Of course, I will, Sugar. But, what in tarnation are you going on about?"

She burst into tears. "You told me no, but I didn't see the harm, and now look what happened!"

"You're not making sense, Giddy honey. I can't understand what you're saying for the blubbering."

She shot her head up at that and Arlen saw a little of the customary fire return to her eyes.

"Out of my way, for goodness' sakes," said Ava as she pushed her way to the front. She handed Giddy a tall glass of clear liquid. Giddy took a sip and coughed.

"It's medicinal...to settle your nerves."

Arlen was stunned. "Ava Corbridge, is that moonshine?"

"If I say it's medicine, then it's medicine, Arlen Well, and you have bigger fish to fry!"

Arlen pinched the bridge of his nose. "Miss Giddy, if you've recovered yourself, would you kindly explain what you meant? What mistake did you make?"

Giddy took a larger sip from the cup, then took a deep breath. "These city boys---outsiders---wanted to hunt our land on the west side of the lake, but Riggs told them no. I didn't see the harm in them getting a few quail and they offered a large donation to the festival---you know the money's going to fix the roof of the schoolhouse---so I said they could. And now they shot Niralya, and Wandalene took her own life because I stripped away her festival duties, and, oh--- I'll never forgive myself!"

She sobbed into her husband's chest as he patted her on the back.

Mr. May cocked his head to the side. "I'm confused. Are you saying it was a hunting accident?"

"If that's what Miss Giddy says, then it must be so," said Nova. "It's nobody's fault, really. Just an accident and those hunters are long gone."

Arlen interjected. "Except that's not what happened."

Giddy stopped crying. "Wh---what do you mean?"

"Mrs. May was not shot with a hunting rifle. The hunters had nothing to do with it, therefore neither did you, Miss Giddy. I hope that puts your mind at ease."

She pulled a handkerchief out of her husband's shirt pocket and dried her eyes. "That does, Arlen, thank you. Though I wish you'd told me sooner and hadn't been so cagey. I've been a bundle of nerves all week!"

She took another slug of moonshine and passed the glass to Ava who refilled it from a pocket flask.

"Well, that's that," said Nova. "I guess we'll never know what happened to poor Niralya."

"Oh, we know, Miss Green," said Arlen. "She was shot with a pistol at close range and then rolled into the ditch."

Mr. May winced.

"Begging your pardon, Mr. May," said Arlen. "But the time has come for plain speaking. Your wife was murdered with a handgun that belonged to Ms. Brackett."

Nova gasped, "Are you saying Wandalene killed Niralya and then couldn't live with the guilt? That's awful!"

"No, Miss Green. I'm saying that someone took Ms. Brackett's gun and shot Mrs. May. Someone who stood to benefit financially from Mrs. May's estate."

Arlen stared pointedly at Mr. May who looked around at the crowd. "Benefit? The only ones who benefit are me and Wandalene---and the tenants in the east cottages."

"How do the tenants benefit, Mr. May?"

"The will gives them a grace period of free rent plus the right to buy their homes outright at a discount depending on how long they lived there. Niralya's lawyer explained it to me when I asked him if we could sell them off. Worthless rock hard land and houses always needing repairs. Good riddance."

Mr. Zader pushed his way to the front. "Is that true? We can buy our homes?"

"Did you not know about that, Mr. Zader?" asked Arlen.

"First I'm hearing of it. But I'll take that deal."

"Oh, it's true," said Mr. May. "The lawyer wants to come out Tuesday morning to bring the papers and explain it all, if that suits you."

Mr. Zader broke into a wide grin. "That suits me just fine, sir!"

"So, wait a minute," said Giddy, her words starting to slur. She drained her glass and smiled benevolently at Ava. "That's good medicine, Ava honey."

"My grandfolks swore by it," said Ava. "Never sick a day in their lives. Until they died, of course."

"I think that's enough, uh, medicine," said Mayor Hutton. "What were you going to say, Sugar?"

"Oh, yeah, let me see," said Giddy. "I remember now. If the tenants didn't know about the will, then they had no reason to hurt Mrs. May. And if someone took Wandalene's gun, then the only other person who benefits is Daxton. Is that what you're saying, Arlen?"

Nova gasped. "That's ridiculous, Giddy Hutton! How dare you say such a thing. Dax would never take Wandalene's .22 much less shoot Niralya. That's drunken crazy talk! We'll sue you for slander, won't we, Dax honey? Why we'll own this town when we get through with you high and mighty Huttons!"

Mr. May held up his hands. "Calm down, Nova. I don't know what Miss Giddy is talking about, but I certainly don't have money to waste on lawsuits."

Nova turned to face him. "What do you mean? You have your inheritance, don't you?"

"Yes, but Niralya put my share in trust. It will be dribbled out to me weekly like a kid's allowance. I'm not spending it on lawyers. Where's the fun in that?"

Giddy giggled and then burped. "You'll spend a pretty penny on lawyers if Arlen arrests you. I'm just saying."

Nova's eyes spit fire at Giddy. "He's not going to get arrested because he didn't do anything! But even if he does need a lawyer, he can pay for it with his own money."

"I can?" Mr. May looked puzzled.

Nova huffed. "For goodness' sake, you can use the money you won on the lottery. There must be a couple of million right there."

"I forgot about that. Yeah, that's gone. Pro tip for you, never play out-of-state games. Pretty sure they're rigged."

Nova's mouth dropped and her face drained of color. "You---you imbecile! Are you telling me that after all I've done for you, you're broke? Broke?"

"I'm not destitute or anything, but my next wife will have to be loaded. And not believe in prenups."

"Why you---!" Nova lunged at Mr. May and began to throttle his throat. He screamed shrilly as Gavyn and Truly pulled the irate woman away.

Rose deftly handcuffed her, and Nova turned her fury on her. "Take these off me right now, Rose Tern! You little---!"

"Now, now, Nova. I understand wanting to strangle the man, but we can't have that, can we? This is for your own good."

Arlen decided he'd given her enough rope. "Nova Green, you're under arrest for the murder of Niralya May and the attempted murder of Wandalene Brackett. You have the right to remain silent---"

"I'm not worried, 'cause you can't prove a thing," she sneered, then paused. "I had nothing to do with that tea. Wait. What do you mean attempted? Isn't she dead?"

"Fortunately for you, she's alive. Now, as I was saying, you have the right to remain silent---"

Mayor Hutton interjected. "Giddy's right, Arlen, you sure are cagey. You had us all thinking Ms. Brackett was a goner. Sly fox!"

The villagers who had watched the spectacle in stunned silence now broke out into chatter as the relief over Ms. Brackett being alive flowed through the crowd. Arlen noticed even Direberry was smiling and patting his neighbors on the back.

Arlen held his hands up to try to quiet them, but to no avail. Suddenly, a shrill whistle pierced the room. All eyes turned on Ava at the podium.

"Can y'all quiet down, please, and let Chief Well finish reading Nova her rights? Do you want a killer to be cut loose because y'all can't keep your traps shut for two minutes? I swanny!"

The room went silent, and all eyes were on Arlen. He finished the formalities, then Truly and Rose transported Nova to the police station in the city. The festival meeting was postponed to the next evening due to the excitement and the fact that Giddy was now indisposed.

Gavyn and Olivia stayed with Arlen at the station to write the reports. Ava bustled around the conference table with cups of coffee.

"No dinner for us, Ava?" asked Arlen.

"You caught the killer, so y'all can get your own supper from now on."

"That's fair, I guess. Although we do have a few hours of reports to write."

They stared at each other. Arlen blinked. "I'll bet the young people are hungry."

Ava narrowed her eyes at him. "Calling my bluff, are you? Getting smart in your old age. Nate and I put the break room back to normal. There's fried chicken, mashed potatoes, and greens plus blackberry tart for dessert. Help yourselves."

"Thank you. Join us, at least for a cup of coffee."

"I will because I want to know how you were so sure it was Nova. She may be right. I don't know how you're going to prove she did it."

"Olivia, do you want to answer that?"

Olivia nodded. "I was recording the festival meeting the whole time and kept the camera and mic on both Nova and Mr. May. She slipped up at least two times. She said Mr. May would never take Ms. Brackett's .22. How did she know it was a .22? Chief Well only said it was a pistol; he never said what caliber."

"That's right," added Gavyn. "Then, she said she had nothing to do with the tea that Ms. Brackett drank. How did she know that the tea is what almost killed her? We didn't let that fact out either."

"The thing that tipped us off in the first place," said Olivia. "Was the photograph of the tea bag that had the sedatives in it. It had been opened and then closed with perfectly spaced hand stitches, which are Nova's trademark. Rose recognized the stitching from the quilt she bought at Christmas."

"I'll give her that," said Ava. "The woman is a hussy, but she sure can quilt."

The next morning Arlen sat alone in the incident room proofreading their reports. He gave Truly the morning off, and Gavyn and Rose returned to their carpentry and landscaping jobs.

Ava brought in a fresh bouquet for the center of the conference table. "We got some good news."

"Oh? What's that?"

"After consulting with her attorney, Nova decided to plead guilty to all charges in exchange for the prosecution taking the death penalty off the table."

"That is good news. That means I can set these reports aside and take the rest of the day off."

"Why would you want to do that, I wonder?" Ava thumped the almanac next to Arlen's laptop.

Arlen had the good graces to look sheepish. "I've got to at least try for that trout and the book says today's a good day for it."

"There's plenty to do around here. Plus, I forgot, the mayor and councilman are waiting for you out front."

"What do they want now? And how's Miss Giddy?"

"Giddy's fine and raring to go for this week's festival. Guess my tonic gave her some pep. Mind you be at the festival meeting tonight since you ruined the one yesterday."

"I caught a killer!"

"True, but now we're having to divvy up Nova's duties and make up the lost time. It's a mess."

"If that's all they want, you can handle that."

"Nice try, Arlen Well. They also want to discuss the lake litter issue that you brushed aside."

"Again, I was chasing a killer."

"You can't rest on your laurels when the community needs you."

"Sound like an issue for the whole village to tackle, not the peace officers. You can tell Chesley and Riggs that from me."

"Tell them yourself. They're waiting on you."

"Unfortunately, that's not possible. I'm going fishing."

"Not today."

"Yes today."

They stared at each other. Ava blinked. "Fine. If you can catch a killer, I 'spect you can catch a trout."

"I appreciate that."

Ava walked away muttering, "Whether you can cook it is another story. I swanny!"

———

Thank you for reading *Mrs. May Is Well and Truly Dead*, the first novella in the Well and Truly Murder Mystery series. If you enjoyed your time in Hutton Village, please leave a review and share your thoughts. Follow Sandy C. McKee on Amazon to be notified the next time Arlen and his team find a victim who is well and truly dead.

Made in United States
North Haven, CT
25 May 2022

19527813R00075